A KILLING IN KENNETT SQUARE

by

MARYELLEN WINKLER

A Killing in Kennett Square
Copyright 2023, Maryellen Winkler
All rights reserved.

ISBN
979-8-9888079-0-2 (paperback)
979-8-9888079-1-9 (eBook)

Published by
Maryellen Winkler Productions
Wilmington, Delaware
U.S.A.

DEDICATION

To F. B.

ACKNOWLEDGMENTS

I would like to thank my friend, Donna Moe,
my First Look Editor; Grace Spampinato of Scribbulations,
my Editor; and Andie Chalfant of Chalfant Graphics
for all their invaluable expertise and advice.

As deadly as the plague

As pervasive as the cold

Greed seeps in unbidden

And ices up the soul.

-mew

CAST OF CHARACTERS

Emily Menotti	Customer Service Trainer at Mirety Bank
Bob Bowie	Human Resources Manager, Emily's Boyfriend
Catherine Bowie	Bob's Mother
Shay Dinsmore	Activities Coordinator at L'Automne
John Dinsmore	Shay's Husband
Edward Weir	Director of L'Automne
Tess Tuesday	Receptionist at L'Automne
Tina Tuesday	Tess's Twin
Rawley Bingham, Sr.	Resident of L'Automne, Catherine's Friend
Rawley Bingham, Jr.	Son of the Above
Nichole & Harold Drago	Residents of L'Automne, Friends of Catherine
Lord Johnston	Chef at L'Automne
Stanley Cubbage	Maintenance Man at L'Automne
Winnie Fields	Nurse at L'Automne
Mike & Joaquin	Trashmen
Jimmy & Elijah	EMTs
Detective Bianca Cortez	
Detective Jake Hudson	
Felicia Fyk	Training Director
Lark Pettet	Credit Training Manager
Nora	Hospital Nurse
Doctor Singh	Hospital Doctor
Zoe	Emily's Cat
Letty Penn	William Penn's Daughter
Mosely	Catherine's Dog

CHAPTER ONE

MONDAY, OCTOBER 29, 2001

It started like every homicide starts—with a dead body. But this body was not just any dead body. This was the corpse of Shay Dinsmore, the biggest busybody in Kennett Square, Pennsylvania.

The Friday evening before, she had told her husband John, while he slowly finished his meatloaf, about the furtive goings on of one of the nurses and her boyfriend who seemed to visit at odd hours. Once, she even thought she'd seen the flash of cash between the two. Heading to her car, she had seen them close together whispering in the parking lot. She was practically salivating to tell someone. So the next person she saw was her husband, home from his job putting in Mrs. Wilson's new septic system. John Dinsmore didn't care about the titillating tête–à–têtes at L'Automne where his wife was employed as Activities Coordinator. But he was a patient man and listened anyway.

On this dreary Monday morning, Shay looked older than her forty-plus years. The person who found her noted that the woman was mostly skin and bones with her long hair pulled back so that not a strand of her mousy brown mane could hide her pasty face. Her eyes were brown also, not a warm brown but an empty, dirty brown, the color of rainwater in the garden. Now, those eyes were cold and blank.

She wore a gray polyester pantsuit circa 1978 and taupe knee-high stockings. Her shoes, and her dignity, were nowhere in sight.

The world-weary sergeant who viewed her lying in the dumpster behind the Walmart on Route 1 recognized her immediately. The stench of her and the flies was something he would never forget. "Shay Dinsmore," he said. "You finally got what you deserve."

It had been raining lightly in the early dawn when the local trashmen found her. They noticed a suspicious human-shaped object in the blur of their bin-cam, so they halted the arms that lifted the bins and gently lowered them down so that Mike could climb out of the cab and inspect the shape.

Mike looked no farther than the face of the figure laying amid Styrofoam cartons and dirty baby diapers. "Call 911," he shouted up to his partner Joaquin. "We've got a dead body."

Stella, the 911 dispatcher, asked Joaquin, "How do you know she's dead? Have you tried to resuscitate her?"

"I wouldn't know how to do that," said Joaquin. "Better hurry."

Hurry, they did. Groggy and cursing, fire and rescue volunteers rose from their warm beds and converged on the Kennett Square fire station on Dalmatian Street. Jimmy Healy woke the sleepy neighborhood with his siren as he guided the emergency rescue van onto Route 1. Not a car was in sight on the four-lane highway, an eerie sight in itself. Overhead sodium vapor lamps lit up the wispy fog and added to the ghostly atmosphere. The earthy odor of local mushroom houses penetrated homes and vehicles alike, the signature aroma of Kennett Square, Pennsylvania.

Jimmy and his shotgun pal, Elijah, the Amish kid from Lancaster who had left his parents' farm ten years earlier for the less quiet life of Kennett, examined the body for signs of life. They found none.

"Who in God's name would want to hurt this poor little woman?" asked Elijah.

"Half the town of Kennett," said Jimmy. "She had something on everyone. A lot of people will rest easier tonight knowing Shay Dinsmore is dead."

"Will anyone mourn her?" asked Elijah as they waited for the police to arrive.

"Her husband, but he might be more relieved than anyone. No one liked Shay. No one...except the director of L'Automne. Rumor is they were doing the nasty in his office late at night."

"How do you know this?"

"Same way I know everything, my wife told me. I can't wait to get home and tell her the body is Shay's."

The wail of a police cruiser was heard in the distance and quickly closed in.

Standing by, Mike hurriedly called to Joaquin, "The Mounties are here" He nodded to a sergeant. "Good morning, sir."

CHAPTER TWO

Three Days Earlier
Friday, October 26, 2001

"I have some bad news for you," Bob told Emily. They were cuddled up on Emily's sofa watching *48 Hours* on TV. A multicolored Afghan, a hand-me-down from Emily's grandmother, was stretched across their knees. Emily kept the thermostat at sixty-eight degrees to save on the electric heat; the kitchen and dining room were dark behind them in Emily's narrow townhome.

"Are the markets down again?" Emily asked.

"Actually, no. They're up today. Despite the continuing economic worries since September 11, the markets seem to be rebounding. My news has to do with our bank."

"Lay it on me," Emily teased. "I'm too comfortable to be worried about much right now."

"I know you've been operating on your own for the last few months without a Training Director or Training Manager. You're meeting the new ones on Wednesday. They're having orientation classes on Monday and Tuesday."

"Darn," said Emily. "I've been enjoying so much freedom. All I've had to do these days is track class attendance. Where are the new guys coming from?"

"The Bank eliminated the Training Department in the Dover office. You'll be inheriting their management team."

"Does that mean our department might be eliminated some day?"

"Couldn't say. I'm not privy to those upper-level management decisions."

"And why not?" she shot back. "I thought the illustrious Bob Bowie was better informed than this."

"You may think me illustrious, but the bank does not. Thank you, though, for the vote of confidence."

"Have you met them?"

"No. All I can tell you is that it's two women. I'll meet them on Monday for orientation. You'll get to see them on Wednesday."

"I guess I better be prepared to explain our manual to them and hope they won't want me to redesign the whole customer service training program."

"That's usually what these types do," Bob said soberly and frowning. "They like to justify their existence that way. But you'll do fine. You always do."

"No, I don't. You know me. I have a problem with authority."

"You always do what I ask you to do," he said, smiling. "Besides, I'm always there to bail you out."

"I don't want you to bail me out. I'm not a maiden in need of rescuing. I want to succeed on my own merit."

"Understood," Bob replied and kissed her. His kiss was warm and tender, and Emily breathed in his cologne, a musky, masculine scent that always aroused her. But, this time, Bob did not seem interested in going further.

After a moment, he leaned away and asked her, "Do you have any plans for the weekend? Will we be seeing Melinda and Elvis?"

"Not this weekend. They're in New England visiting Melinda's old friends."

"So if you're free, will you come with me to visit my mom tomorrow?"

"Tell me again where she lives." Emily now leaned in closer to take advantage of his warmth. She was too pleasantly settled to get up and look for a sweater.

"L'Automne Senior Living, off of Kaolin Road near Kennett Square," he said. "It's about a half an hour from here." Sensing her need for warmth, Bob put a protective arm around Emily's shoulders.

Emily gratefully snuggled closer. "How old is your mom?"

"Eighty-five."

"Does she like meeting new people?"

"Yes. I've told her a lot about you."

"Then I'd like to meet her. What time do you want to pick me up?" Emily smiled at Bob. She was happy to think they'd be spending the next day together.

"I'll be here at ten-thirty so we can arrive between eleven and eleven-thirty. We can have lunch with my mom, either there or we can go out. We'll let my mother decide." He retrieved his arm and pulled the Afghan from his knees, piling it on top of Emily. "Don't get up," he said and then kissed her quickly and stood up. "I've got to go. See you in the morning."

"Okay." Emily sighed and listened as Bob let himself out. She looked around at her cat, Zoe, who was curled up asleep on the other side of her. Zoe's inky fur shone softly in the half-light from the TV. "Time for bed," Emily whispered.

As Zoe padded upstairs behind her, a tired Emily willed her body up the steps wondering how many other women in tiny houses were also making their way upstairs to remove makeup, brush their teeth, and crawl into bed alone. Bob rarely spent the night. He preferred her to stay at his place where he could have a nightcap and not worry about driving. But that left Zoe alone all day *and* all night.

Standing in her nightgown, Emily studied her face in the mirror and thought she'd pretty well weathered the ravages of fifty-three years. There were no gray strands as yet in her blonde hair, but the dark circles under her eyes had become a permanent feature. She sighed and dragged her feet into the bedroom.

She sat in bed with the covers pulled up and took out a notebook. Every night since her divorce, when she was alone, she wrote in her gratitude journal. Recording what she was grateful for was something she had learned from the *Oprah Winfrey Show.* At first, writing had helped her overcome those lonely nights when she missed the companionship of her ex. Ten-plus years later, the strategy still worked. "Good health," she wrote, "caring friends," "Zoe," and ended with "Bob." These were her most important sources of happiness. Then she wrote the less consequential things: "white wine," "dark chocolate," and "butter pecan ice cream."

Emily put down her notebook and pen and shut off the light. She patted the bed to tell Zoe she could jump up and join her; she loved the sound and feel of Zoe's soft, warm body. Zoe landed at her feet and then walked pit-a-pat up beside her. Next, Zoe made a circle and settled down inside it. Emily felt like she was not alone. Millions of women were sharing that same feeling that cool Friday night, curling up in their beds with only their pet for company, feeling that, at least, this small furry animal cared about them.

Emily considered what a sad world it would be without pets.

She fell asleep quickly, unaware of the consequences of a simple visit to an elderly parent awaiting her on the morrow.

CHAPTER THREE

Saturday, October 27

Bob arrived on time, as always, Saturday morning, and Emily invited him in while she found a jacket and grabbed her purse. Bob smiled as he reached down and petted the cat, telling Zoe Emily would be back later.

It was late October, and the trees outside Emily's townhome had changed from soft, shining greens to bursts of red, gold, and orange, a herald for the coming winter. Nature saved her most vibrant colors for her stunning finale. The bejeweled trees distracted the viewer from the neighborhood's neglected homes and litter in the streets. Eyeing the trees, Emily thought, *We seek out beauty unconsciously and respond to it like children offered candy.*

Bob drove as fast as the moderate traffic would allow him, skirting Newark on the East and following North Chapel Street out to Paper Mill Road. Then he took Route 7 North through an upper middle-class suburb of minimansions hastily constructed with identical brick facades and vinyl siding. Once they crossed the Pennsylvania state line, the houses thinned out and the trees closed in. Bob drove carefully along the narrow lanes of Kaolin Road, which came perilously close to the steep banks of the Red Clay Creek before the road turned left to cross the creek and climb up modest hills to Kennett Square. Shortly before the town limits, Bob turned left down a fresh macadam lane that rolled over a grassy rise. A small red sign with gold letters announced "L'Automne."

"This is magnificent!" Emily remarked as they approached a grand stone edifice that resembled an English country home. From the top of the drive, Emily could see three stories of tall mullioned windows dominated by six gables, three on each side of the dark wood entry. The roof was crenellated, providing a hint of castle romance. Vermillion drapes graced each window, giving the structure an air of elegance. Behind those drapes, one could imagine women in long gowns and high gloves gossiping among themselves in the drawing room, while men in tuxedos had a leisurely whiskey in the study. Emily pictured herself in a black cocktail dress, sipping a vodka martini. Remembering all the British mysteries she'd watched on TV involving country houses and murder, the thought of gliding through those elegant rooms suddenly made her shiver.

"I'm feeling just a little spooky," she said. "Like there might be a dead body in the library."

"I don't think so," Bob laughed. "Although you might come across one in the nursing wing."

After parking the car, they took the shaded walk from the lot to the front entrance. Broad cement steps led up to a pair of heavy glass doors beneath a thick wooden arch. Once inside, Emily felt a rush of warm air. They entered a wide room with a tall counter on their left and a spacious lounge area on their right. She was disappointed to find that the inside walls were not dotted with massive family portraits of bygone ancestors staring down menacingly on the latest generation of wealthy scoundrels. She found, instead, a sunny room filled with sofas and soft chairs, the walls painted a graceful eggshell tint. An elderly woman sat on a pale blue sofa, reading a newspaper. Soft classical music wafted in the background. Emily detected a scent of lavender.

Dominating the center of the room were the mansion's original wide marble stairs. They gleamed like polished clouds, illuminating shining paths to the upper and lower stories. Small signs in gold leaf print were mounted on the white marble railings with black arrows indicating up to the "Residences," down to the "Activities Room," and straight ahead to the "Dining Room." In a far corner there was an elevator and metal steps to an office that overlooked the lounge.

"I'm here to see Mrs. Bowie," Bob told the young receptionist. She wore her pale blonde hair pulled back in a ponytail with loose tendrils falling across her brow and ears; she looked as if she'd just gotten out of bed. Her alabaster skin gleamed with the health of a young woman, and the skin around her sapphire blue eyes was smooth showing no laugh lines or dark circles. Her black sweater was pulled tight over wide shoulders and just a hint of breasts, emphasizing the impression of health and athleticism. She looked up at them with a smile radiating kindness and sociability. Oddly, she was seated so low that she could barely see above the counter. Her nameplate read "Tess Tuesday."

"Please sign in," she replied, pointing to the oblong book on the countertop. Her voice was soft yet animated—almost musical.

As Bob and Emily complied, Tess said to Emily, "I don't believe you've been here before, Miss. I'll need to see your driver's license to verify your identity."

Emily was a bit surprised. Did she think Bob would bring someone with a questionable background to see his mother?

At her hesitation, Tess added, "HIPAA rules. Sorry."

Emily frowned. She didn't think HIPAA rules extended to visitors in assisted living facilities, but perhaps this small lie was an easier way to ask for identification. Since the destruction of the Twin Towers in Manhattan, everyone seemed to be extra cautious.

She dug in her purse for her wallet, extracted her license, and handed it to Tess. As she did so, she could see over the top of the counter and noticed that Tess was seated in a wheelchair. A wave of compassion instantly replaced Emily's annoyance. The effort of propelling a wheelchair also explained Tess's muscular arms.

Tess handed back Emily's license and said, "I believe Mrs. Bowie is in her room. Will you be staying for lunch? I need to alert the kitchen staff if there will be guests."

"I don't know," Bob replied. "I have to ask Mom."

"I'll tell the kitchen two extra. If you don't eat here, it won't be a problem. Better too much than too little. The kitchen staff will be glad for leftovers." Tess picked up the phone to make the call.

"Thank you," Bob said. He turned to Emily and pointed to the elevator across the room. "Let's go," he said.

The elevator was whisper soft as it whisked them up to the second floor. Once there, the doors opened silently, where Bob and Emily found an elderly resident in a fuzzy bathrobe hunched over her walker and waiting patiently.

As Bob and Emily exited, an aide rushed up to the resident and gently touched her shoulder. "Let's put on some clothes, Mrs. Gunn. You know the rules. We must wear street clothes in the dining room."

"Oh, I forgot," Mrs. Gunn said, brushing imaginary crumbs from her plush pink robe. The aide gently helped her turn around, and they started back down the hall together.

"Seems like a very nice place," Emily commented as they made their way in the opposite direction, their steps softened by thick blue carpet. The walls were sparkling white with framed Wyeth prints of the Chester County landscape. Scattered along the wall were wing-backed chairs next to small tables holding tall china lamps that lit up the long passage.

"Here we are, number 204," said Bob, stopping and knocking gently on the door.

The door was quickly opened by a tiny woman with pure white hair. She wore a white turtleneck top with gray wool slacks. A soft aquamarine scarf that matched her eyes was carefully arranged across her shoulders. It was her gracious smile, however, that one warmed to first.

"It's so good to see you, dear," she said to Bob and raised her arms for a hug. After embracing, she said, "Please come in. And who is your friend?"

"This is Emily Menotti," Bob answered. "She's the woman I've been talking about. She's very special. Emily, this is my mom, Catherine Bowie."

"Hello, dear. Let's have a hug." She raised her hands to Emily's shoulders, giving Emily a moment to refuse in case she wasn't the hugging kind. But Emily was and quickly bent over to wrap her arms around Mrs. Bowie, both extending their embrace for a few seconds to enjoy the mutual affection and goodwill.

"I can tell she's special," Catherine said, letting Emily go and ushering them into her compact sitting room.

"I'm so happy to meet you, Mrs. Bowie," Emily said, noting how her blue-green eyes matched Bob's.

"Please call me 'Mom' also," she said to Emily. "Would you like something to drink?" Catherine started to walk to her small kitchenette, only five steps away from the door.

"No, thank you," Emily replied.

Catherine retraced her steps.

"We're here to have lunch with you," Bob said. "I'd like to take you out if you feel up to it."

"Yes, dear, I'd love to escape for an hour or two. This is a lovely place, but the menu is limited. Can't be helped when you're trying to please a hundred people."

Suddenly, someone knocked on the door and opened it quickly, not waiting for the invitation to enter.

"Mrs. Bowie," said the thin female with hair the color of tree bark that matched her polyester pantsuit. Holding up a Lucite clipboard, she strode in and stood in the middle of the sitting room. Frowning, she announced, "Don't forget you're signed up for the bridge tournament at three this afternoon."

"She'll be here," Bob answered.

"I'm sure you remember Shay Dinsmore, Bob," Catherine said, nodding at the woman. "She's the Activities Coordinator here. Shay, this is my son, Bob, and his friend, Emily."

"Very nice to meet you," Shay replied, not offering her hand.

"Are you from Kennett?" Shay asked, eyeing Bob. She unashamedly examined him head to toe. "I don't recall seeing you around town."

"Shay knows *everybody* in Kennett Square," Catherine explained.

"No, we're from Wilmington, Delaware," Bob replied.

"My, your hair is thin," Shay commented. "I do hope you wear a hat when you're outdoors. You might get a sunburn."

The personal remark shocked Bob. *Is my hair that thin? Is this woman really rude enough to point it out?* "I wear a hat in the summer months," he replied defensively.

Poor Bob, Emily thought. *Who wants attention drawn to their shortcomings?*

"Well, I'm glad to hear that," Shay said. Turning to Emily, she continued, "And you, Miss, have quite an interesting pattern of beauty marks. A person could play tic-tac-toe on your left cheek."

Emily was mortified and too flustered to respond. This awful woman was highlighting her and Bob's imperfections.

Before Emily could respond, Shay continued, "Now, Mrs. Bowie, I won't bother you anymore." She headed for the door. "Don't forget!" She smiled, turning her head to admonish them as she let herself out. The smile that accompanied her parting words seemed genuinely heartfelt. For the briefest moment, happiness sparkled in her eyes. Then she was gone.

"I'm sorry, dear. Shay means well," Catherine said as she reached for a gray blazer from the coat closet. "She is a bit of a pest."

Bob took the blazer from her and held it out for his mother to slide her arms in. He was still irked by the woman's remarks and had nothing kind to say about her, so he said nothing.

"People here do have memory problems," Catherine explained as she adjusted a gold leaf pin on her lapel. "Are you alright, dear?"

"I'm fine," Bob said, recovered now. "My ego isn't too bruised, and I'm always happy to meet any of the staff here so I can be reassured that you are being properly cared for."

"I can fend for myself, dear," she said as she motioned for Emily and Bob to follow her to the door. "But it's nice to hear you say that. Where shall we eat?"

As they were leaving the apartment, Emily noticed a large dog, a black Labrador Retriever, curled up on a plaid cushion in a wicker basket.

"Oh, you have a dog," Emily said and reached forward to pet the dog on the head, but as her fingers touched his fur, she noticed that the eyes were plastic, and her fingers quickly felt that the fur was fake. Embarrassed, Emily withdrew her hand and said, "He looks so real."

"Doesn't he?" Catherine replied. "That's Mosely. He was a gift from my dear son," she said, nodding at Bob, "when my real lab, Mosely, passed away. He does his best to keep me company."

"Mom wouldn't move into assisted living as long as the dog was alive," Bob explained. "When he finally died from old age, I convinced her to move in here."

"And thanks for drawing my attention to him. I always say good-bye to him when I leave." Catherine walked over to the dog, bent down, and scratched his head. "Back in an hour or two," she said to him.

Emily was quietly amused at Mrs. Bowie's treating the stuffed toy like a real animal, but she said nothing.

Catherine straightened up and said, "Off we go." She ushered them out the door and locked up.

"Where would you like to eat?" Bob asked again as the trio headed down the hall to the elevator.

"Do you think it's too late in the season for a crab cake sandwich?" Catherine asked. "We rarely have crab, probably because it's so expensive."

"How about the Kennett Square Inn?" suggested Bob. "The one on State Street. I think they have crab on their menu."

"Sounds wonderful," his mother said. "I haven't had a good crab cake sandwich in ages."

The elevator arrived, and they rode in silence to the main floor. Catherine went to a row of mailboxes to see if she had any mail while Bob and Emily signed out.

Tess called out, "Mr. Bowie, is this yours?" She held up a gold money clip about three inches long and one inch wide. The initials *RB* were engraved in a florid script. "One of the staff just turned it in. Since your initials are *RB*, I thought it might be yours."

Bob took it and turned it over in his hand. The clip was only slightly tarnished with use. Then he handed it back. "No, I'm sorry, I don't use a money clip."

"Thank you anyway," Tess said. "I guess I'll give it to the director for safekeeping."

As Bob and Emily started toward the door, a gray-suited gentleman entered and walked across the lobby to the elevator. Emily recognized him immediately as Rawley Bingham, Jr., an embarrassing part of her past she needed to make amends for.

She quickly asked Bob, "Can you and your mom wait a minute? I have to speak to someone." She caught up with the man and touched his arm.

"Rawley? It's Emily Menotti. You remember me?"

Rawley spun around and frowned at her. Emily noted that Rawley looked almost exactly like his father had looked when she dated him thirty-plus years ago. He was taller and bald now, with dark intelligent eyes.

"Not likely to forget you," he finally said. "What are *you* doing here?"

"I'm with my boyfriend visiting his mother," Emily explained. "His mom is Catherine Bowie."

"I'm on my way to see my father. He's waiting for me."

"Stay a minute, please. For years I've been hoping to run into you. I owe you a huge apology."

"What for?"

"For not asking you to my prom back in high school. I thought I was being cute and clever, like Patty Duke on *The Patty Duke Show*. Remember how she was always engineering situations to help someone out?"

"What's that got to do with me? You didn't play fair. I asked you to my high school prom, and then you dumped me and had one of your friends ask me to your high school's prom instead. And you did this at a party where everyone could see what was happening. I was totally humiliated. Now you're telling me it has something to do with Patty Duke?"

"I'm so, so sorry, Rawley. You were always a gentleman when we went out. You were a kind and considerate date. I was a stupid teenage girl. Will you let me explain?"

"I'm kind of in a hurry."

"It'll just take a minute. Our paths may not cross again. The girl who asked you to the prom, she was a good friend and didn't have anyone to go with. I didn't want her to miss out on her prom night, and you were such a nice guy that I thought you might take her and you both would have a good time. I just assumed we would stay friends afterward. The problem was, I should have asked you about it before I did anything, but I thought you would have said no."

"Depends. The worst part was that you pulled this trick on me in front of others."

"I know, and I have felt badly about it ever since."

"Well, it's a little late now," Rawley said. "Although I guess you did me a favor because I found out what kind of person you really are. Does your boyfriend know about this?"

"No. It happened so long ago; I don't think it's relevant to who I am today."

Rawley continued to frown but was now at a loss for words. He felt too confused to know what a correct response to her explanation would be. "I'm going to see my father," he finally said and turned away from her.

Emily let him go. Her shoulders sagged, and her stomach ached. Her apology had not gone like she had hoped it would. She rushed back to Bob and his mom, smiling to hide her feelings. She was heartsick that her apology had gone so wrong.

"Are you alright?" Bob asked as he held the door for the two women. "How do you know the Binghams?"

"I'll tell you another time," Emily replied softly. "Right now, I just want to get to know your mom."

"Don't let Shay bother you, Emily," Catherine said as she settled in the front seat of Bob's SUV, tactfully ignoring Emily's conversation with Rawley Jr.

Emily obligingly climbed in the back.

"She's a little overzealous in performing her duties," Catherine continued. "If you let her, she'll get your mail for you and pay your bills from your checkbook. I'll bet she'd even scrub your back when you took a bath. My friend, Rawley, lets her do all sorts of things. I'm almost afraid to ask him for details. I doubt she has many scruples."

"Why would they let her work here if her ethics are questionable?" Bob asked.

"She's the director's sister-in-law. It would take a major scandal to fire her. I remember that, once, a former resident complained about her, and Shay then decided to give him the full Shay treatment. He couldn't find his mail; he lost laundry items; and we all suspect she tampered with his pills. He finally chose to move out rather than put up with her."

"Would you like to move?" Bob asked.

"Oh no. I'm very happy there. For whatever reason, Shay seems to respect me and leaves me alone. I do keep my good jewelry and checkbook locked up in a metal box, but I would do that anywhere. Don't worry, dear. I have wonderful friends at L'Automne, and I don't want to leave them."

CHAPTER FOUR

Downtown Kennett Square was only a short ride from L'Automne, but the one-way streets made it necessary to travel east on Cypress, then north on Willow, then west on State Street until they found an on-street parking spot.

When they arrived at the Kennett Square Inn, Emily admired the colonial white brick building with tall windows and pale green shutters. Bob was pleased to find that there were still a few tables available. The dining room had a traditional Americana look with Windsor dining chairs and tables draped in white cloths. Each table was adorned with a small pewter lamp. The yeasty smell of baked bread enticed them to take a deep breath and smile.

Their waitress had an easy job. After they were seated and given water, all three ordered the crab cake sandwich and iced tea.

"How are the meals at L'Automne?" Emily asked, turning to Catherine. She couldn't quite bring herself to address her as "Mom" at this early stage of their acquaintance so she just omitted saying, "Mrs. Bowie." "What sort of dishes do they serve?"

"Oh, the usual institutional fare such as roast chicken, roast turkey, and roast beef." Catherine laughed. "They're not too big on fried foods. We usually have fresh vegetables with dinner, but everything tastes a tad overcooked."

"I thought you had a wonderful chef there," Bob said.

"Oh, we do. His name is Lord Johnston, but he's not really a lord." Catherine giggled.

Emily warmed to her even more.

"He's British, and his parents must have had a quirky sense of humor. He creates marvelous dishes, but by the time we get them, I think they've been reheated in the microwave. However, he does make a delicious crème brûlée sometimes for dessert."

"Do you eat many mushroom dishes?" Emily asked. "I know Kennett Square is the Mushroom Capital of the World."

"About once a week, we're treated to mushroom soup or a mushroom omelet. Lord's not heavy-handed with the mushrooms.

I don't care for them. I can usually scrape them off or pick them out."

The three stopped talking when their sandwiches arrived. Emily found hers to be delicious, with large chunks of white crab and no noticeable filler. She sighed with contentment and saw that Bob and his mother were similarly enjoying their meal. It wasn't until all were feeling beyond full that conversation started again.

"Your receptionist seems young for a job at a senior living facility," Emily said.

"Oh, Tess is a gem," Catherine responded. "The interesting thing about her is that she had an identical twin named Tina."

"Had? Did you ever meet the twin?" Emily asked.

"No, but Tess has told us all about her. She said that Tina ran off with her boyfriend. It's a rather tragic story. The two girls lived together in a house near Newark, Delaware. Then Tina met a man who came from Mexico. They fell in love.

"Suddenly one weekend, Tina announced she was leaving. Tess said Tina and her boyfriend eloped to Mexico. Not long after, the boyfriend called to say that Tina had died in a boating accident and that her body could not be found."

"How sad," murmured Emily.

"Do you know why she's in a wheelchair?" Bob asked.

"She told us she has multiple sclerosis. She only came down with it a year or so ago, a little before her sister left for Mexico."

"Did her twin have it too?" Emily asked.

"No, just Tess."

"What a story!" Emily said. "You'd think one twin would stick around to help out the other if she were disabled."

"I asked Tess about that—discreetly, of course," Catherine smiled. "She said she was glad Tina had found love, brief though it may have been. Tess's van and her home are all set up to accommodate her wheelchair, so she has no problems getting around."

"I certainly admire that," Emily responded. She imagined she would want someone, preferably male and good-looking like Bob, to live with her and help out if she were disabled.

"I don't suppose Tess gets a chance to date. Her illness might frighten off a lot of guys."

"Well," Catherine said sadly. "There was a rumor that she and the director were having an affair before she became ill. But once she got sick, he dropped her cold."

"Yet he let her keep her job?"

"I guess to fire her would have been too cruel. It has to be difficult to find work if you have MS."

They let the subject drop as the server appeared and asked who wanted dessert. All three declined. The server put down the check, and Bob quickly covered it with his hand.

"This is my treat, Mom," he said. "It's such a pleasure to see you and have lunch together."

"Can I leave the tip?" she asked.

"No, this is all mine," he said, giving the server his credit card.

"Please excuse me," Emily said and rose from her seat. "I'm going to visit the ladies' room."

Emily wound her way through the tables and headed back toward the bar where she assumed the restrooms would be. She was startled to see a young girl about twelve years old with dark blonde hair pulled back in a pink ribbon. She was seated at the bar with a bowl and spoon before her. Emily glanced at her quickly and wondered if she were the daughter of a server or bartender waiting for her parent to finish the lunch shift. She didn't think about the girl until she passed her again on her way back to the table. Emily noticed the old-fashioned dress the girl was wearing; the white cotton fabric had puffy sleeves and was gathered loosely at the waist. The skirt was long enough to cover the girl's feet as she sat on the bar stool, so Emily couldn't see what sort of shoes she had on.

"I like your dress," Emily said, briefly stopping to admire it. The girl looked up at Emily with soulful brown eyes.

"I'm Emily. What's your name?"

"I'm Letty," she replied. "And my dress is a new one from Philadelphia. But you must not speak to me. I'll be punished for talking to a stranger."

"I'm sorry. I'll go," Emily replied and turned away.

"Be careful," the young girl said. "You're in danger."

"What?" Emily asked, turning back around.

"Beware the changeling," the girl said, looking at her with her solemn dark eyes. Then she looked down at her lap.

Startled and unsure how to respond, Emily turned away and rejoined Bob and his mom.

"I just had the strangest experience," she said as she sat down. "I was talking to that young girl sitting at the bar."

"What young girl?" Bob asked, swiveling his head in that direction. Emily turned around and saw that all the bar stools were now empty.

"She was just there; I guess she left."

"I've been watching the bar the whole time we've been sitting here," Catherine said. "My chair faces that way. I never saw a young girl, although I did see you looking at one of the bar stools as if someone *were* there."

Oh no, thought Emily. *Am I seeing things?*

Bob was only too aware of Emily's history with paranormal experiences, but he wasn't ready to explain it to his mom. He decided distraction was his best move. "Let's go," he said. "The bill's paid." As he stood up and began to help his mother with her jacket, he added, "We have to get you back to L'Automne for your bridge tournament."

Stepping outside, the three blinked in the bright sunlight. As their eyes adjusted, they saw the sky was a startling blue. After the Inn's dim lights and close atmosphere, the air felt cool and clean, fresh and energizing. They walked quickly to the car.

When they returned to L'Automne, Catherine said, "Just let me off at the door, dear. It's so beautiful; I think I'll take a quick walk around the grounds. I need to walk off that heavy crab meat."

"Okay, Mom. Love you," he added as she let herself out.

"Love you too, son. Talk to you later."

As Bob drove away, Emily said, "Your mom is wonderful. You're lucky to have her."

"I know," he replied. They didn't speak of the girl in the white dress who was or was not there.

On the ride back to Emily's house, Bob asked, "What's up with the Bingham guy? Looked like you two had an intense conversation."

Emily began, "I had to apologize to him for something that happened in high school."

"Do tell."

"I went to an all-girls high school, and my friends and I usually dated guys from a nearby boys school. The prom was always a special event. I was dating Rawley at the time and he invited me to his school's prom."

"Did you go?"

"Yes. His was earlier in the spring then ours."

"And you invited him to yours, right?"

"I should have. But I had a close friend, Monica, who was never asked out on dates, and I didn't want her to miss out on the prom."

"I'm guessing she had no one to ask."

"Right. So I decided she should ask Rawley to go. He was a very nice guy and I thought she would have a good time with him."

"What did he think of your idea?"

"Well, that was the problem. I didn't tell him."

"No?" Bob took his eyes off the winding Kaolin Road long enough to look at her in disbelief.

"No. I asked someone else to the prom instead." Emily paused for a moment to take a breath. It was difficult remembering how hurtful her behavior had been.

"Then I had a party where I invited a bunch of people including my prom date, Rawley, and Monica. At the party, I talked mostly to my prom date and ignored Rawley. Monica hung out with Rawley and later in the evening asked him to the prom."

"So Monica knew of your plans, but not Rawley?"

"Yes." Emily hung her head, still feeling ashamed of her behavior.

"I would have been pretty angry if I'd been Rawley. Why did you do this? He was *your* boyfriend."

"After I thought about it, I was afraid he wouldn't agree with my plan for Monica to attend the prom. But I went ahead with it anyway."

"You weren't in love with him."

"I liked him a lot, but no, I wasn't in love."

"Where did you even get such a harebrained idea?"

"I used to watch this TV program called *The Patty Duke Show.* Do you remember it?"

"Vaguely, but I never watched much TV when I was a teenager. We only had a small black and white set."

"I wanted to be like Patty Duke. She was continually pulling pranks on people, always with the best intentions. I wanted Monica to go to the prom. I thought I was doing the sort of thing Patty Duke would do."

"Did Rawley take Monica to the prom?"

"He did. But he hasn't spoken to me since."

"I can't blame him. And the boy you invited, who was he?"

"It was someone I already knew. I hadn't been dating him on the sly, though, if that's what you're thinking. I had gone out with him the summer before on one or two dates. And he was a second or third cousin too."

"Doesn't excuse it."

"No, it doesn't, but it took me years to realize what a position I put Rawley in. It was wrong of me. All wrong."

Bob could hear the regret in her voice, but he couldn't stop thinking how upset he would have been in Rawley's shoes.

"Did you keep seeing the other guy?"

"No, he made it clear he already had a girlfriend. He was just someone for me to take to the prom so Rawley could go with Monica."

"It does seem like a thoughtless teenage thing to do."

"I've been hoping for years that I would run into Rawley to apologize. So when I saw him today, I had to do it."

"How did he take it?"

"Not well."

"I'm not surprised."

"Me neither. But it's done." Emily sighed, sounding more tired than relieved.

"What are your plans for me?" Bob joked. "Any girlfriends you want me to date?"

"I wouldn't foist you on anyone! Come on, don't you have stupid teenager stories?"

"Mine just involve booze and cigarettes. Pretty typical adolescent stuff."

"I don't believe you. But I'll let it slide for now."

Bob didn't respond. He was busy thinking about the women who were part of his life. One talked to stuffed animals, and the other talked to ghosts. He was glad he was the rational one.

CHAPTER FIVE

Catherine walked leisurely around the grounds of L'Automne, admiring the manicured lawn, well-kept shrubbery, and carefully pruned trees. She'd had her doubts about moving to an assisted living facility, worried it would be like high school with cliques of residents hogging the best activities and excluding those who didn't meet their standards of wealth and taste. Luckily, she'd been wrong. There were a few unfriendly residents, but most had invited Catherine to join them in their book club, at lectures, or on outings to restaurants.

When Catherine approached the desk to sign herself in, she noticed Tess and her wheelchair were not there. Turning around to see if she was elsewhere in the lobby, she saw her friend Rawley Bingham, Sr. in the lounge reading the local paper. Rawley was in his late eighties and had a bald head that gleamed like polished porcelain. He was tall and stout, his cardigan sweater buttoned tightly across his chest.

"Oh, Rawley, how are you?" she asked and walked over to sit beside him. "Do you know where Tess is?"

"No, I haven't seen her. Did I tell you that I lost my money clip? I usually keep it in my dresser, but now it's missing."

"I thought I saw Tess with it earlier. I assume she would have given it to the director. She asked my son if it was his."

"Well, she said she did give it to him, but the director says she never did, and he doesn't have it. Now I'm out two hundred dollars."

"Do you really carry that much money around with you all the time?"

"Of course! We men need our 'walking around' money as my father used to say."

"Do you think someone at L'Automne might have taken it?"

"Most of our friends here are pretty well off. I doubt they would need it. I'm suspecting one of the staff."

As he finished speaking, Lord Johnston came in with his

stained white apron still tied around his waist. He walked right up to Rawley.

"Guv, I've just spoken to the director. Neither I nor my staff took your money clip. I would swear on the Bible that they would never do such a thing." Lord Johnston ran his fingers through his short waves of graying hair. "I probably would have given it to Tess if I'd found it."

"It's okay, Johnston, don't worry. I don't suspect you or your staff. And that was a marvelous lunch we had this afternoon. I love your apple blintzes."

"Thank you, sir. I'll let you know if I hear any of the kitchen staff talking about found money."

"I'd appreciate that."

Lord Johnston wiped his hands on his apron, turned, and hurried back toward the kitchen.

When he was back among his friends—his friends being the gas stove with eight burners, the four-door oven, and the large walk-in refrigerator—Johnston heaved a sigh of relief.

"Any of you ladies know anything about Mr. Bingham's missing money clip?" he asked the waitstaff, who were starting to clock out.

"No, Mr. Johnston," the four said in unison.

"You let me know if you hear anything," Johnston said. "Can't have us being suspected of thieving."

"We will," they answered in unison again, then they made a hasty retreat for the back door.

Mr. Johnston was worried, nonetheless. *Trouble always flows downhill*, he thought, *and a man of color and his team were always at the bottom.*

CHAPTER SIX

At two-fifty Saturday afternoon, Shay Dinsmore knocked on Catherine Bowie's door.

"One moment," Catherine shouted. After a few seconds, she came to the door and opened it.

"Just brushing my teeth," she explained, without inviting Shay inside.

"Bridge tournament in ten minutes," Shay said.

"Thank you, dear. I'll be there soon."

Shay hurried off.

Catherine finished brushing her teeth and checked that she'd left no lights on or water running in the sink. She saw her purse on the coffee table and placed it in the bottom of her clothes closet. She wouldn't need it downstairs, but she didn't want it in plain view in case the cleaning staff came in while she was gone. Then she put on her gray sweater, patted Mosely good-bye, and headed out the door. She locked the door behind her even though she thought it was rather silly that they were required to do so. The cleaners, nurses, and director all had a set of keys. The only people kept out were other residents and stray family members looking for a relative's room.

She took the stairs down to the lower level, where the Activities Room had been set up with a dozen square card tables.

The bridge hands were already laid out, cards facedown, awaiting the tournament's start, alongside paper pads and pencils for scoring. It would be a duplicate tournament, with the same bridge deal played at each table and the participants moving from table to table hoping to outperform the previous card players.

Catherine met Shay Dinsmore in the hallway. Shay's hair was now disheveled, and her blouse was half out of her skirt. Catherine felt obliged to speak to her, "You should tuck your shirt in," Catherine whispered.

Shay stopped abruptly and blushed deeply. "Thank you," she murmured as she attended to her blouse.

Catherine smiled and wondered if Shay's désordre had anything to do with what went on in the director's office.

Shay recovered quickly after fixing her clothes. She showed Catherine a list of where each person would be seated. "You're at table five," she said. "It looks like your partner is already there."

Catherine made her way around the chairs to her table and found Rawley seated and smiling up at her. She took the chair opposite his and asked, "How are you, partner? Ready for a challenge to our title?"

"Ready and willing," he smiled.

"Have they found your money clip yet?" Catherine asked as she settled into the padded folding chair.

"No, but my son is coming later this afternoon to speak to the director. He's all upset. I shouldn't have told him about it this morning. Now I'm going to have to listen to a lecture from him about being more careful."

"I'm so sorry, Rawley. I don't tell Bob much myself. The nurse has tried to give me the wrong pills twice, but luckily I'm still sharp enough to know what I should be taking. If I told Bob about it, he'd insist I move. Would you like me to take a look around your apartment with you? A second pair of eyes is always helpful."

"They've messed up my pills once or twice also. But I think we'd run into the same issues someplace else. I like it here too. Johnston's cooking is better than average. So yes, you could help me take a second look. There's another worry I have too. Can I stop by your apartment tomorrow and show you some papers? They're copies of ledger pages that Shay gave me. I'm having some memory issues. I know there's something not right about the figures, but I can't tell what it is."

"What kind of ledger pages?"

"Copies of the bookkeeping accounts. Shay knows I was once a CPA, so she asked me to take a look at them."

"Whose accounts are they?"

"This place. L'Automne's. Oh, here comes the opposition." As he finished his sentence, two residents sat at their table.

"Hi, Nichole. Hi, Harold," Catherine and Rawley said together. Catherine added, "How are you this afternoon?"

Nichole and Harold Drago were in their eighties and long-time residents of L'Automne. Both had soft white hair in almost identical short-cropped styles. Nichole's face was still smooth and dewy.

Catherine wondered how she had managed to keep it so young looking. She couldn't see any evidence of a face lift, so she figured Nichole was blessed with the right genes. Harold's skin was ashen with red blotches. Catherine thought he didn't look well. She would ask Nichole about it in private sometime.

The Dragos had retired to L'Automne after selling a chain of miniature golf courses at various beaches in and around Wildwind, New Jersey. Catherine had played at some of them in her younger days. The courses were ambitious, with lifelike jungle animals and real waterfalls gracing the fake-turf fairways. Nichole had confided to Catherine that they had started out quite modestly with one miniature golf course in Wildwind Crest and then slowly acquired nine more over twenty years. Patting her carefully coiffed hair and posing stylishly in a silk blouse and black leather pants, she liked to call herself The Queen of Miniature Golf. Her husband, who favored gray wool slacks even in summer and highly polished black shoes, merely smiled at her as if at a prized possession.

"We're ready to take on the champs," Harold said as he pulled out his wife's chair. Then he took his own and looked around the room as if assessing the competition.

"We have some bad news," Nichole said. She frowned and showed just a hint of a wrinkle around her mouth. "We just discovered a thousand dollars missing from our bank account. It happened sometime last month, and we only discovered it now when we got our bank statements."

"How did it happen?" Rawley asked. "Are you missing any checks?"

"Yes," Nichole said, shaking her head sadly. "Someone wrote a check to 'Cash' for a thousand dollars. So that means someone from here, right?"

"I'm so sorry," Catherine said. "Where do you keep your checks?"

"Well," Nichole frowned, "I know I should keep them locked up, but it's so inconvenient. I do leave them out sometimes on the desk."

"Have you told the director?" Rawley asked.

"Yes. He asked us not to go to the police until he did his own internal investigation."

"We'll give him a week," Harold added. "Then we'll call the authorities."

"I'm missing my money clip with two hundred dollars," Rawley said. "I've also spoken to Weir, and like you, I'll go to the police if it's not found in a few days."

"How about you, Catherine?" Nichole asked. "Are you missing any money?"

"Not so far. Here's Shay at the podium. Let's talk about this later."

"Good idea," Harold said. Then, he commented, "Good turn out."

The other three followed his gaze around the room to see the tables rapidly filling up.

Shay Dinsmore rapped on her portable microphone to get everyone's attention.

"We'll be starting in a moment," she said. "You all know the rules of duplicate bridge. Send someone up to me from your table when you're done playing the hand, and when everyone is finished, I'll announce the table changes. For instance, a couple from table one will move to table four, etcetera, etcetera. Any questions?"

Nichole Drago raised a hand with carefully lacquered red nails. "Will there be refreshments?"

"Yes, dear. The waitstaff will bring bottles of water to each of you, and halfway through the tournament, we'll have a break with cocktails and snacks. Anything else?"

There were no more questions.

"Very well, pick up your cards and begin."

As the room quieted, Shay slipped away to take care of other business.

CHAPTER SEVEN

Rawley Bingham, Jr. arrived at L'Automne at four-thirty in the afternoon. "How are you, Tess?" he asked as he signed in.

"Just wonderful, Mr. Bingham," she replied. "Your father is in the Activities Room playing bridge."

"I'd like to speak to the director," he said. "Is he in?"

"Let me check," Tess replied. She picked up the phone and pressed the extension button. "Mr. Weir? Rawley Bingham, Jr. would like to speak to you. Are you free?"

"Send Bingham up," Weir replied.

"He'll see you now," Tess told Rawley. "You know where the office is?"

"Oh, yes. Thank you."

Rawley Bingham, Jr. was a carbon copy of his father, including his shiny bald head. At fifty-three, he had fewer wrinkles and a firmer step, but there was no doubt what he would look like in thirty years. He walked across to the far right corner of the room and up a short flight of metal stairs. These led to the director's office, which sat on a platform overlooking the lounge. The modern stairs and platform office had been added in the 1980s when the private home was converted into a senior living facility. The small office had a glass wall to survey the floor below, but Weir usually kept thick drapes pulled across them. Rawley knocked lightly on the door.

"Come in" he heard and opened the door.

Mr. Weir's office was austere and bereft of plants or paintings to soften the décor. Only flat white paint adorned the walls. The furniture was Danish modern in a dark wood that stood out against the colorless walls. Several certificates and plaques were displayed atop a wide filing cabinet.

Mr. Weir had the frown lines of a forty-something man, yet he had muscles like a much younger one. His curly ginger hair was short and soft, his eyes pale gray. Rawley recognized that women would find him handsome, but each time he saw Weir, he was startled by the thought that Weir looked more like a stevedore than a director. Weir's air of health and vitality appeared out of place with his turned-down mouth and catchphrase "Of course there's a problem."

He sat in his chair with his legs straight out and his shoes propped on his empty desktop. He wore a black golf shirt and khakis. He nervously bobbed his right foot, clad in a brown tassel loafer, up and down, up and down.

"Have a seat," he said softly. "How can I help you?"

"My father lost his money clip this morning," Rawley said. "He had two hundred dollars in it. I'm concerned it was stolen."

"Yes, your father alerted us when he came down for breakfast. I've discussed this with my staff, and a search has been made. We weren't able to find it."

Rawley frowned. He wasn't satisfied with this answer.

Weir hastened to add, "All our staff pass security reviews before they're hired. I'm hesitant to accuse one of my people."

"Could it have been someone from the outside, like a visitor or a delivery person?"

"We haven't had many visitors today, and the delivery people never go into the residence area."

"Have you contacted the police?"

"I was hoping it would show up so that wouldn't be necessary."

"And has it shown up?"

"No."

"Do you think *I* should contact the police?" Rawley raised his voice in frustration.

"I wish you would hold off on that. Give us some more time to search. I know your father is still pretty sharp, but our residents often complain of someone stealing their things, then those items turn up a day or two later. The elderly are very forgetful."

"Okay, but I want you to know I'm concerned. I'll let this wait until Monday." Rawley rose to leave.

"Thank you," Mr. Weir responded. "I'll be in touch."

Shay had disappeared from the tournament for a few minutes to talk to Tess. On her way through the lobby, she ran into Rawley Bingham, Jr.

"Mr. Bingham, how are you this afternoon?" she asked.

"Not happy," he replied. "But I'm glad I ran into you. What do you know about my father's missing money clip?"

"I only know that he lost it. Has it been found?"

"No, and I'm quite upset about it."

"Well, these things happen in a retirement community. The elderly are so absent-minded. But I'll speak to all the staff again and ask them if they've seen or heard anything."

"My father has been a resident here for quite a few years. I don't recall anything like this happening when the previous Activities Coordinator was here. In fact, since you've been working here, I've heard of three or four such incidents of missing money."

"None of those were your father's."

"No, but I'm beginning to wonder if you have anything to do with them." Rawley knew this was a wild accusation, but he was upset to think his father had been victimized.

"You don't understand the situation here."

"I think I do understand it, and it doesn't look good where you're involved. There could be consequences...like your job."

Shay was shaking with anger now. "Mr. Bingham, I am the director's sister-in-law. Don't even think you can get me fired." Shay hadn't meant to say this, but it slipped out even as she thought, *This man has no idea how muddle-headed these old folks are. He should be grateful his father has such a beautiful, well-run facility to live in.*

Rawley, meanwhile, was eyeing Shay with suspicion. Who better than the Activities Coordinator to know when residents would be out of their rooms? "I've just spoken to the director. I'll wait to see if he can find my father's money before I make any decisions."

"You do that," Shay spat out. "You'll have to excuse me now; I've a room full of seniors to see to."

"Don't forget what I've said," Rawley responded grudgingly. He walked away, seething inside with anger at Shay and with frustration at his inability to resolve the situation that afternoon.

In the dining room, Lord Johnston was placing small vases of flowers on the dining tables. Inadvertently overhearing most of the exchange between Rawley Jr. and Shay, he shook his head and smiled. Johnston harbored no love for Shay Dinsmore. She was forever finding fault with his staff and how he ran his kitchen. The girls' skirts were too short, or the gravy was too greasy. He kept smiling as he wiped his hands on his apron and walked away.

Shay returned to the bridge tournament and watched as the

couples played additional hands of bridge, desperately trying to smother the panic roiling inside her. She couldn't wait for the card games to be over.

Around five-thirty, the last scores were handed in, and Shay spent a few minutes tallying them up. Pleading budget cutbacks, Shay explained that the prizes were not the gift certificates for restaurants and merchandise they had been in the past. Then she awarded the first-, second-, and third-place prizes. "This year's first-place prize is graciously awarded to Catherine Bowie and Rawley Bingham...a bottle of Moet Champagne. Second place, to Nichole and Harold Drago...a bottle of Kendall Jackson Chardonnay. Third place, a bottle of Gallo Merlot, goes to Peg and Steve Castaneda."

At six on the dot, Tess Tuesday rolled her wheelchair to the elevator and rode it down to the lower level where she could smoothly exit to the employee parking lot. Being handicapped, she had the first space closest to the building. *So blessedly convenient*, she thought as she powered the chair up the short ramp and through the side door of her van. She pulled herself up into the driver's seat and was about to start the engine when Shay walked up to the van and tapped on the window. She was holding an envelope in her hand. Tess rolled down her window.

"Have you taken a look at those ledger pages I gave you?" Shay asked.

"Haven't had the time," Tess replied. "What do you care if Weir's taking a little extra for himself?"

"My sister lives in near poverty. I want to know where the money goes."

An uneasy alliance existed between these two women of different ages and personalities, but such relationships were necessary when reporting to the same boss.

Sighing, Shay continued, "I found this mail on the floor near the entryway, and it's addressed to you. Since it's from the Social Security Administration, I figured it was important. I thought you should have it right away."

Tess took it from her hand. She recognized what it was but also noticed that it looked damaged. Had this happened in the post office, or had Shay opened and resealed it?

"Yeah, well, thank you," was all Tess said. She put the envelope in her purse and started to roll the window back up, then thought better of it. She was so tired of Shay prancing around L'Automne like it was her private kingdom and she was the queen in charge of it all. Now was Tess's chance to let Shay know what she suspected.

"You're here late," Tess said. "And Weir's still here too. Nice opportunity for you two to be alone." Tess gave her a knowing leer. *Maybe this will put a dent in your smug smile,* she thought.

Shay's eyes shot open wide, and she reeled back as if she'd been slapped.

"You know I barely tolerate that piece of garbage my sister married."

"Really?" was all Tess said, and she started to roll the window up.

Shay put her hand on the window to stop her. She leaned in close. "I have my suspicions about you too," she whispered.

"Please take your hand off the window," Tess said, hoping the sudden huskiness of her voice didn't give anything away.

Shay took the hint and turned away silently.

Tess waited and steadied her nerves. *What does Shay know? Is anyone safe from this busybody?*

CHAPTER EIGHT

Shay was back at L'Automne; she had returned after a quick trip home to fix dinner for her husband. After parking her car at the rear of the building where kitchen deliveries were made, she went slowly and carefully down the hallway to insure she wasn't seen or heard, then ascended the steps to the lobby.

She looked around quickly to see if anyone was in the vicinity. A nurse's aide at the desk was reading a *Vogue* magazine. Seeing no one else, she climbed the stairs to Weir's office, knocked softly, and opened the door.

Shay stood there for a moment, waiting for Weir to notice her. When he did, he only said, "We need to return Bingham's money clip." He pulled a cigarette from a pack of Marlboros on his desk and lit it with a blue Bic lighter. After taking a puff, he added, "We didn't plan that one well enough."

"I never thought it was a good idea," Shay replied. "Too complicated—taking the money and giving the clip to Tess, telling her I found it. I'm glad Tess gave it back to me without asking too many questions." Although she wanted a cigarette, she didn't ask Weir to give her one. *He's so selfish. He never offers.*

"I know, but I needed the funds. And now we've got Bingham's son all riled up."

"I've got a plan," Shay said. "Leave it to me. But let's have a drink first."

Weir reached down to open a cabinet where he kept vodka for Shay and Scotch for himself. He took out the near-empty liquor bottles and two glasses.

"I want a stiff one," Shay said.

"My pleasure," Weir replied.

CHAPTER NINE

Sunday, October 28

Sunday morning after brunch, Catherine and Rawley were walking together back to their apartments when the director appeared with Shay Dinsmore at his side.

"If you don't mind, Mr. Bingham," he said to Rawley, "I'd like to take a quick check myself to see if I can find your money clip somewhere in your apartment. I have Shay here with me as a witness. I want to be sure that the search done by the staff yesterday was thorough."

"No problem," Rawley replied. "But you should know Catherine and I did a second search just before we came down for brunch. We didn't find it." Turning to Catherine he said, "Will you stay while I wait for the director to finish his inspection?"

"Of course," she replied.

Arriving at Rawley's apartment, he and Catherine sat down on his sofa while Shay and Weir entered Rawley's bedroom. He doubted they would find anything. Catherine was equally dubious of what Weir and Shay were doing, but for Rawley's sake she kept quiet.

They could hear Weir and Shay opening drawers and closet doors, knowing they were searching among Rawley's personal effects. Rawley wasn't feeling too pleased with this invasion of his privacy, but he didn't see that he had much choice.

After ten minutes, Mr. Weir returned with the lost money clip in his hand, the engraved initials *RB* leaving no doubt about its owner.

"Is this it?" he asked Rawley and handed it to him to examine.

"It is," Rawley said, shocked. "Here are my initials engraved on it. But the money's gone. There was two hundred dollars in it. Where did you find the clip?"

"Under your pajamas in your bureau drawer."

"I know we checked there yesterday," Shay said. "Myself and the nurse. We went through every drawer and lifted up every item of clothing."

"Is it possible you moved it yourself, Mr. Bingham? Are you trying to cast suspicion on my staff?"

Rawley visibly bristled at the question. "Of course not," he said emphatically. "Are you implying there's something wrong with my mental faculties?"

"No, no, of course not," Weir crooned as if to a small child. "Well, let's not worry about how it got there. Let's just be glad it's found."

"Thank you, I guess," Rawley said. "But I'm very sure I didn't put it there. And I'm still out two hundred dollars." He frowned in confusion as he turned the money clip over in his hands.

"Let's go, Shay," Weir said. "Mr. Bingham, be sure and call your son and let him know we found it." The director then left, with Shay right behind him.

"Do you think he fell for it?" Shay asked Weir.

"Not sure," he answered. "But that's the best we could do."

"Wow, this is weird," Rawley said to Catherine. "I would never put my money clip under my pajamas. And the money is still missing. I really don't know what to think about it. My brain hurts when I do. It's hard to admit, but I've noticed that a lot lately. I try not to think too hard about anything."

"Maybe you should get a small safe, Rawley. You could put your money in it at night."

"I keep forgetting that the staff sometimes comes in and checks on us at night. Do you have a safe?"

"No, I only just thought of that. Ask your son to pick one up and bring it next time he visits. Maybe I'll ask Bob to get me one too."

"I think I'll do that. I want to get away from here now. Would you like to go to a restaurant for dinner? Sunday night here is usually sandwiches anyway, since they give the kitchen staff time off to be with their family."

"I'd like that. Why don't you come by my apartment around five."

Catherine left and returned to her apartment. The first thing she did upon entering was to walk over to Mosely and scratch the top of his head. "Did you miss me," she asked him. Mosely responded with a snuffle and a nudge of his nose against her thigh.

Catherine found the Sunday paper and thought she might read for a while but decided to pay some bills instead. Picking up the stack of Saturday's mail, she placed it on the coffee table and retrieved her checkbook, a pen, and stamps.

Most of her mail turned out to be junk: insurance company solicitations, realtors wanting to buy the house she had already sold, and postcard advertisements for restaurants and sub shops. When she opened her Visa bill, she was shocked to find a balance of over $400. Catherine only used her credit card for dining out and occasional mail-order purchases from Talbot's. Her card number was also on file with the office at L'Automne for charging incidentals like hair and nail appointments in the salon that operated on the premises two days a week. Her bill was rarely more than one hundred dollars.

Examining the details, she saw a water bill for $99 and an electric bill for $250 had been charged to her card. She knew that was impossible. Her monthly fee here at L'Automne covered all utilities. She decided to call the credit card company and dispute these charges. But how did they get there?

Catherine thought she'd better check that her card was in her purse. She got her purse and pulled out her wallet. Her credit card was missing. *Thank goodness I didn't offer to pay for lunch,* she thought. *I would have looked foolish and upset Bob. He would have thought I was getting senile.*

Catherine tried to remember if she had used the card after the last charge on the bill. It was weeks later, and she could have used it for the hairdresser or a lunch out. Her only other choice was to think that someone had stolen it. She checked the pouch where she kept her paper money and saw untouched fives and tens. Would a thief have left paper money behind? Perhaps a waitress held on to it the last time she used it to pay for lunch. *I need to call the credit card company right away!* She quickly found an 800 number on the bill and called it.

Catherine reported the incorrect charges.

The customer service representative couldn't have been nicer. "And do you have your credit card in your possession?" the representative asked.

"No, I can't find it. I think a waitperson at the last restaurant I visited must have held onto it when I used it to pay."

"I'm going to cancel that card and send you a new one with a new number," the representative explained. "You should have it in a week to ten days."

"Does it have to take that long?"

"We could send it by overnight mail, but that will cost twenty dollars."

"No, that's alright. I can wait. And what will happen to those charges?"

"Since you've explained that you didn't authorize them, we'll remove them. The fraud department might call you to verify those charges aren't yours. Sometimes people forget, and then their memory is jogged later on and they remember making them."

"That won't happen with me. I don't own a house anymore. I don't get water and electric bills."

"Understood. Someone will be in touch in a day or two. Is there anything else I can help you with today?"

"No, thank you."

"Then have a nice day." The call ended.

Catherine decided she should let Bob know about her credit card being stolen. She called his home telephone, but when it went to voicemail, she didn't want to leave a message. She would tell him about it next time she saw him. She decided to read the Sunday newspaper until it was time to go out with Rawley.

Someone knocked at her door. Glancing at the clock, she saw that it was 4:45. She set down the paper and went to the door, finding Rawley with a bunch of white papers in his hands.

"Hi, Catherine," he said. "I know I'm early, but I wanted to show you these."

"Come in, Rawley," she replied. "Is this what you were talking about yesterday?"

"They're copies of my copies, which are hidden back in my room, underneath a section of the carpet. I'm afraid to leave anything out after what happened with my money clip."

"What is there about these papers that has you so worried?"

"Here, take a look and tell me if anything looks funny."

"Well, come in and sit down. This will take a few minutes. Would you like something to drink?"

"No, I'll wait until we get to the restaurant. Please take a quick look now."

They both sat down on the sofa, and Catherine began to examine photocopies of a ledger book. The top of each page was titled "Expenses" and was followed by a date. Below were subtitles: "Staff wages," "Food," "Cleaning," "Utilities," and "Miscellaneous." Under each subheading were the expected entries of staff names, food deliveries, the name of the cleaning service L'Automne used, and the various utilities such as water, heat, gas, fire protection, and media. By far, the longest list of payees was under "Miscellaneous," items like "new carpet for room 305" and "Sent flowers to family of deceased, Dolly Hixson." These expenses were expected. The $7500 amount for Arts, Crafts, and Decorations seemed high. But the Thanksgiving and Christmas holidays were coming; that could be a reasonable amount.

"What exactly am I looking for?" she asked him after leafing through half a dozen pages.

"I don't know. Everything seems legitimate, but I get a funny feeling when I look at these numbers. I'm a retired CPA! I'm used to looking at columns of numbers, but something doesn't sit right about these. Damn, I wish I didn't feel like I was losing my mind sometimes."

"Do you think there are bogus expenditures? Did Room 305 get new carpet?"

"Yes, it did. I checked that out. And a new client named Dolly Hixson did die shortly after she came here. I just can't put my finger on what's wrong."

"Well, if it'll make you feel better, I'll keep these and look at them again later. I'm hungry now, if you don't mind. Let's go to dinner."

"Of course," he said. "But let's be safe. Put those papers away. Don't leave them laying out for the staff to see. Especially if Weir should pay you a visit."

"I'll put them under the paper lining my lingerie drawer. No one ever goes in there," Catherine said with a sad smile.

"Maybe someday I'd like to look in there," Rawley whispered and gently kissed her on the cheek.

"Maybe someday I'll let you," Catherine replied and gently returned the kiss. "Stay here. I'll be right back." She got up and disappeared into her bedroom. Rawley heard her open and close a drawer. When Catherine returned, she carried a light jacket with her.

"I'll tell you about my credit card problem on the way," she said. They walked out together, shutting the door behind them, but not before Catherine patted Mosely on the head and told him she'd be back in an hour or two.

As Catherine locked the door, she smiled and thought, *As if locking this will do any good.*

CHAPTER TEN

At eight o'clock Sunday evening, Shay Dinsmore sat in her car in the Walmart parking lot and surveyed her purchases. Wednesday would be Halloween, and she had picked out additional decorations for L'Automne with funds from her checking account. Weir had been adamant that the budget didn't have any leeway to allow ceramic jack-o'-lanterns, spooky cobwebs, or cloth scarecrows. The only items allowed were fresh pumpkins and implements for carving them. There would be a pumpkin carving contest after lunch on Halloween.

Shay had given Lord funds to purchase a variety of small hobby knives and paints. But with *her* money, she had bought a cloth scarecrow and a cloth witch, each life-size with needlework detail on their faces to approximate a human visage. Now sitting in her back seat, the witch wore a tall black hat of a satiny material and a coarse dark dress that billowed out to her shiny black shoes. Next to her was the scarecrow, composed of real straw bound together with twine where there would have been joints and dressed in a red plaid shirt and blue overalls. Shay thought both figures were quite well-done. She'd also bought small baskets decorated with orange and black bows that she would fill with miniature candy bars. She planned to distribute these on Halloween to each apartment while the residents were at dinner.

Shay rolled down the driver's side window and opened the glove compartment. Reaching in, she felt for her cigarettes and quickly pulled one from the package. After lighting the cigarette, she sucked in a long generous lungful of smoke and let it out with a sigh. Smoking was her only guilty pleasure, other than the occasional frantic lovemaking she shared with Weir.

As she approached forty, Shay found she could no longer eat dairy and chocolate without getting a forty-eight-hour migraine. It was so unfair, she thought. She was now forty-plus years old, in a loveless marriage with no grandchildren, and she couldn't even relieve her boredom and depression with a bite of chocolate or an ice cream cone. So cruel. Cigarettes did not trigger a migraine, and for that, she was grateful. She inhaled deeply on her cigarette again, feeling her muscles tense with each inhalation and then relax as she exhaled. It was her form of meditation. She blew the smoke out the open car window. That's when she saw him.

He'd just pulled up in a parking place two spots over, a young man with straight cornflower hair and long, lean limbs. As graceful as a cat, he lifted one leg and dismounted from his motorcycle. Even though it was dark, he wore mirrored aviator sunglasses. He stood up and stretched his arms to the sky. Shay was enthralled by his performance and his beauty.

The young man, who looked to be in his twenties, must have felt her staring and turned to look at her. Embarrassed to be caught gawking, Shay put her head down. When she looked up again, he was gone.

Shay's heart beat faster while the rest of her body went limp. The man reminded her of someone she had dated in her twenties, a man her husband never knew about, a man who played in a rock band and would telephone her every time his road tour came to Philadelphia.

She considered how her friends might think her longings for him were sexual, but they weren't. When Shay had met this man, she was newly married and already bored. One night when Shay had been out drinking, the lead singer had singled her out of the audience in a local bar and introduced himself. Back then, she'd had a body she could flaunt with cropped tops and low-rise jeans. Her mousy hair and been long and full of golden highlights.

She and her husband constantly fought about money, and on one particular night, she had walked out in the middle of another endless argument and had gone to the bar to drink and dance. The lead singer's halo of pale hair, his dark eyes and stature, and his deep voice and poetic vocals awoke in Shay the oddest feeling. Shay didn't want, as many women might, to be with him sexually. She wanted to *be* him. She wanted to be a beautiful lean young man who could travel the world with only a few changes of clothes and a guitar. No monthly periods, no looking for a place to sit down and pee, no constraints on her love life. Just the freedom to come and go as she pleased.

Of course Shay couldn't tell him that.

This desire to know him and live his life through his eyes was an aphrodisiac Shay had never experienced. When he asked her to wait until after the show, she'd agreed and followed him up the back stairs to the rooms where the bar housed its performers. The sex was not all that terrific, but it allowed her to feel her skin on his skin and fantasize that *she* was the lead singer in a rock 'n' roll band.

The next afternoon she'd returned to the bar, and he'd taken her for a ride on his Harley. They rode up through the woods where Routes 82 and 100 wound beneath the trees and skirted the Brandywine River. They flew along the blacktop, leaning into curves and accelerating on the straightaways with Shay's arms tightly wound around his waist. She'd felt free; she'd felt alive; she'd felt like life was one long endless possibility.

He left town the next day with the promise of returning, which he did every year for five years until one year he didn't.

All this Shay remembered as she sat in her rusting Chevy and finished her cigarette. A parking lot light flickered high up on a steel pole, the evening darkened, and a light rain began to fall.

Out of the cold mist, the motorcyclist suddenly appeared by her door. He tapped on her window. She rolled it down.

CHAPTER ELEVEN

Sitting in a cozy diner on old Route 1, Catherine told Rawley about her missing credit card.

"We have a thief in our midst," Rawley said. "You need to tell the director."

"I'll do it first thing Monday morning," Catherine replied. "But I hate telling him. It means grilling the staff and having them look daggers at me every time I see them because I've accused them of a crime."

"Don't forget about my money clip," Rawley said. "And the Dragos' fraudulent check."

"But Weir found the money clip in your bureau drawer. Did you forget you'd put it there? I mean, we all forget a lot these days."

"You looked with me Sunday morning. You know it wasn't there. Someone snuck in, took it, and kept the cash. Then they got scared and replaced it. Probably while we were at brunch."

He's right, she thought. *What was I thinking?*

"They're such nice people," Catherine said as she picked at her veal parmigiana. She was thinking it had been the wrong thing to order in a diner. The veal was like rubber. "And they get paid so little," she added.

"That's no excuse," Rawley said, enjoying his roast turkey and stuffing smothered in gravy. "Besides, they'll be a snap to catch. How stupid of them to pay a utility bill with a credit card. The credit card company will have the address for the property, and the director only needs to match up the address with the employee."

"If it *was* an employee. I still think it was taken the last time I used it in a restaurant."

"We'll know by the end of the week," Rawley assured her. "Let's be grateful the credit card company didn't give you a hard time about reversing the charges."

"They used it to pay their utility bills," Catherine mused. "They must have been desperate not to have their services turned off. I almost feel sorry for them."

"I have some more bad news for you too."

"Oh, no. What?"

"Catherine, I understand your son is dating a woman named Emily. Right?"

"Yes. How did you know? I don't recall discussing her with you." Catherine frowned.

"My son ran into her in the lobby. She said she was visiting with your son. What do you know about her?"

"Not much. We went out for lunch. She works at the same bank as Bob. She seems nice enough." She chose not to tell him about Emily's seeing a young girl at the bar that Catherine knew wasn't there.

"Tell Bob to be careful. She's not a particularly kind person. My son told me how she used and embarrassed him in high school."

"In *high* school? Really, Rawley, most girls are a bit silly and unthinking as teenagers. Can we hope she's grown up and wouldn't do anything like that again?"

"I don't know. I'd tell Bob to look out for his heart. She might still be a bit foolish, and he could get hurt."

"Well, I'll mention it to him, but I'm not worried. I was no paragon of virtue myself in high school." That was what she said, but now she *was* worried.

Later that night, Catherine had trouble falling asleep. She was thinking about the ledger sheets but, after a while, dismissed them. *There's nothing I can do about them tonight.* Then she began to worry about what Rawley had told her about Emily. Was Emily a threat to Bob's happiness? She doubted it. And what about her seeing someone who wasn't there at the bar? Catherine wasn't sure where she stood on ghosts. *I've never seen one. Does that mean they don't exist?* The Inn was rumored to be haunted. Perhaps she should get to know Emily better before she made any judgments or said anything to Bob.

Rolling over in bed and adjusting her pillow, she began to relax. Suddenly, she felt something jump on the end of the bed and begin to pad toward her. After a moment, she felt the warm and wet muzzle of Mosely's snout on her cheek. She reached up to pet him.

"My secret love," she whispered to him as he lowered his big body onto the bed beside her. Catherine stroked his soft fur and pulled his warm body closer. Snuggled up next to Mosely, she let go of her troubled thoughts and settled into sleep.

CHAPTER TWELVE
Monday, October 29

At 10 a.m. on Monday, twenty elderly men and women sat in a circle in L'Automne's Activities Room. Nichole and Harold Drago sat side-by-side in chairs spaced six feet apart. It was time for their Chair Aerobics class.

Catherine and Rawley soon joined them, Catherine asking "Isn't Shay here yet?"

"No," replied Nichole. "And you know what else is strange? She didn't come by and knock on our door this morning to remind us to come to class."

"She didn't knock on my door either," Rawley said.

"Nor mine," added Catherine.

A low buzz of voices began as everyone speculated where Shay could be. No one could remember a time when she had been late.

"Perhaps the traffic is especially bad this morning," Harold offered.

"Or she's ill," Rawley said.

They waited fifteen minutes, voices buzzing around them with speculation on where Shay could be. Then people began to leave in groups of twos and threes. Finally only Catherine and Rawley were left.

"I'm going to talk to Tess," Catherine said. "Maybe she knows something."

Catherine left the room and went up the steps that led to the lobby. Approaching the reception desk, she saw Tess on the telephone, a concerned look on her face. As she reached the desk, she heard Tess say, "I'll tell the director to expect someone. Thank you."

Tess set the phone down and looked up at Catherine.

"Shay's dead," she said. Tears began to form in her blue eyes.

"They're calling it a homicide. Can you believe it?"

"Who were you talking to?" Catherine asked.

Before Tess could answer, Weir came through the front doors. He looked paler than usual, his ginger hair uncombed, his eyes more worried. His hand shook as he placed a cardboard coffee cup on the reception desk counter.

"Have you heard about Shay?" he asked.

"Yes, just now," Tess said. "The police called. They're sending someone around to talk to you."

"They called my wife at our home," Weir said. "Poor Shay. She didn't deserve this."

"Did they say how she was murdered?" Tess asked.

"No." He gripped the edge of the countertop to steady himself. "Look, don't bother me with anything this morning. I'll be in my office. Cancel my appointments."

"Of course. Would you like me to have the kitchen send up some coffee?" Tess asked. "You seem quite upset."

"No, no. I've got some here." He picked up the cardboard cup from 7-Eleven. "When the police come, send them up." Weir hurried off, stumbling across the lobby and clutching the railing on the stairs up to his office.

"He's taking it hard," said Tess. "I feel so bad for him."

"She'll be difficult to replace," Catherine commiserated. "I'll tell the others." She kept her thoughts to herself. *Does her death have anything to do with those ledger pages Rawley gave me?* She would miss Shay, but she'd never warmed to her. She did feel sorry for her husband and children.

Catherine and Rawley huddled together in the lounge with some of the other residents, voices buzzing around them with the terrible news that Shay Dinsmore was dead.

Seated close by, Nichole Drago asked her husband, "Do you think we're in danger?"

"Oh no," Harold replied. "Shay could be a nasty person. Her sharp tongue earned her a lot of enemies in Kennett Square. We have nothing to worry about."

"Until one of us dies," Nichole said.

"I don't think anything's going to happen to us," Harold said, trying to reassure her.

Catherine and Rawley were having a much different conversation. It never occurred to either of them that they were in any danger.

"Do you think someone here killed her?" Catherine asked.

"It's certainly possible," Rawley said.

As he spoke, they saw two strangers enter the lobby, walk up to the reception desk, and flash badges. One was a Black male in a gray suit and the other a Latina woman in a blue skirt and black boots. They introduced themselves as Detectives Hudson and Cortez. Catherine and Rawley could overhear them.

"The director is waiting for you in his office," Tess said, pointing them toward the metal stairs on the right side of the lobby.

"Thank you," Detective Hudson said. "We'll need to speak to all the residents and staff when we're finished. That includes you. Is there somewhere we can do that?"

"In the Activities Room," Tess replied and pointed to the marble staircase a few feet from her desk. "Take those steps to the lower level."

"Thank you. Can you get us a list of everyone here?"

"Of course! It's on the computer. I'll have it for you when you're done talking to the director."

"Can you bring it up to his office?" Detective Cortez asked.

"I'm in a wheelchair. See?" Tess pointed downward. The detectives looked over the desk and nodded.

"The elevator doesn't connect with the office. You have to climb those stairs over there." She again pointed to the metal stairs in the far right corner of the lobby. "But I'll have a list for you when you come back. Give me fifteen, twenty minutes to print it out."

"Alright," Cortez spoke. "We'll come back. In the meantime, please assemble everyone in the Activities Room. Let's go, Jake."

Tess picked up the intercom and made an announcement over the PA system that sounded throughout the building.

"Attention, everyone! It's necessary for all residents and employees in the building to come to the Activities Room on the lower level. The police are here and need to speak to each of you. The only ones who are exempt are the residents in the hospital section. However, any staff in that area who can safely attend, should. Please assemble as quickly as possible. Thank you."

Next, she rolled her wheelchair to the elevator and descended to the lower level. She parked herself at the Activities Room door so she could be the first to leave when the meeting was over.

Catherine and Rawley returned to the Activities Room, as did Nichole and Harold, and were soon joined by almost one hundred other residents and about thirty staff. Wearing his stone face, Lord Johnston arrived along with a handful of kitchen help. Next, the maintenance man Stanley Cubbage arrived, wiping his hands on a dirty towel.

In the office, Detectives Jake Hudson and Bianca Cortez were unimpressed by the director and his faltering speech.

"Where were you on Sunday night from six to midnight?" Hudson asked him.

"Here, in my office, working on the books," Weir said. He picked up a pen lying on the desk and twirled it nervously between his thumb and index finger.

"How close were you and the deceased?" Cortez asked.

"Not especially close," Weir said, still twirling. "I was her boss; she was my employee. She's also my wife's sister; that's how she got the job."

"If she's your wife's sister," Hudson said. "Did her husband call you or your wife last night when Ms. Dinsmore didn't arrive home?"

"No, he didn't. But you don't know him. He was probably drunk and passed out by eight. He wouldn't have known anything was wrong until he woke up this morning."

Cortez and Hudson didn't look at each other but didn't need to. Each knew that Weir was confirming Dinsmore had been asleep earlier when officers had knocked on his door with the bad news.

"What about children?" asked Cortez.

"There are only two, and they're both away at college."

This also confirmed what the detectives already knew.

"You're sure she didn't say anything to you about what she was doing last night?" Cortez asked. "There were Halloween decorations in her car. Were they for here?"

"I don't know. I didn't tell her to buy any. We hadn't budgeted for them."

"You don't seem to know very much," Cortez continued, "for a man who was both her boss and her relative. Women like to talk. I'm sure she was at your house for holidays and birthdays."

"Actually, she wasn't," Weir said. "Shay was a difficult person. She was very good at her job because she enjoyed being with people. She enjoyed controlling people. She also enjoyed judging people, and her judgments were never kind. My wife and she had a falling out two years ago over a missed lunch date. My wife forgot to call and didn't show up. Shay never forgave her."

"Can anyone vouch for your being in the office last night?" Cortez asked.

"Well, no. I guess not. Tess, the receptionist, she's not here on Sundays. One of the nurses' aides mans the desk."

"Who takes care of the door if they're away from the desk?" Cortez asked.

"You ring a bell, and one of the nurses' aides will come and let you in. We found that most of our residents stay in on Sunday night. Occasionally we arrange, or rather Shay would arrange, a trip to the theater or a concert. But mostly everyone stays in."

"We can assume that you would have access to a number of different drugs needed for your clients, right?" Cortez asked.

"Yes, but why? I would never help myself to any drugs."

"Ms. Dinsmore was drugged." They didn't add any more particulars. They would leave that for the killer to confirm.

"And you think someone from here stole the drug and used it to kill her?"

"Yes, it's a theory."

"You can check with the nurses. We have a sign-out system to track who takes a drug and who it's administered to."

"We'll do that shortly. What are your home address and telephone number?"

Weir responded, and Hudson wrote down the information.

"Are you married?" Cortez asked.

"Yes. You know that."

"Any girlfriends?"

"No."

"We'll be in touch," she said.

"Please, yes," Weir replied. "I want to know who did this. Shay will be terribly missed."

"Of course," Cortez said, and the two detectives left.

Weir finally put down his pen and reached for his half-empty coffee. After a sip of the now-cold brew, he shook his head. *Thank God that's over with*, he thought. Then he put his head in his hands and began to cry.

In the Activities Room, word had already gone around to everyone that Shay Dinsmore was dead. A few, like Nichole and Harold, still briefly wondered if they were in danger. Most, however, were concerned only with the interruption to their schedules. There'd be no more Chair Aerobics, no bridge tournaments—no fun at all—until a replacement was found. They hoped it would be soon.

A few had personal concerns. Mrs. Gunn was too confused by numbers to write checks for her bills or balance her accounts. Shay had helped her with that. Mrs. Gunn worried who would do it now. Half-deaf Mr. Stanford needed someone to call his children occasionally and tell them how he was doing. Shay had been glad to do that, although sometimes he wondered what they talked about for twenty or thirty minutes.

Shay had been only too glad to insert herself in the residents' lives.

Detectives Cortez and Hudson entered the room and looked out at over one hundred faces turned to them for information and reassurance.

"Is Shay Dinsmore dead?" Mrs. Gunn shouted out. She was seated on the small padded platform attached to her walker. "That's what they're all saying."

"Yes, I'm afraid so," Detective Hudson said, raising his voice and waving his hands so all would quiet down. He was aware that many of the elderly were hard of hearing. He was gratified to see that all eyes were on him and his partner.

"Ms. Dinsmore's body was found earlier this morning, and her death has been ruled a homicide. If anyone has any information that might help us to find her killer, we'd appreciate it if you came forward. We want to know who her friends were and if she had any enemies." A titter went through the crowd. Cortez and Hudson looked at each other. What did that mean?

"How'd she die?" Nichole Drago asked.

"We can't give you any details at this time," Detective Hudson explained. "Those details will help us catch the killer."

"Who's going to replace her?" An anonymous voice arose from the crowd.

"We can't tell you that either," Cortez said. "You'll have to talk to the director."

The detectives waited thirty seconds in silence. No one asked any questions or offered any useful information.

"We ask that everyone stay in their apartments today until an officer has come by to take your statements. We'll need statements from everyone here, even if you didn't know Ms. Dinsmore well."

Hudson frowned, thinking he and his partner were in for more inane questions they couldn't answer, but their words were met with silence.

"Then, if no one has any more questions," Cortez said, "you can return to your rooms or your duties."

The two detectives stood at the doorway and watched the residents file out. Some had dressed carefully in soft blouses and crisply ironed slacks. Others had worn sweatsuits, women displaying embroidered flowers or kittens, men with bold stripes down the sleeves and pant legs. A few shuffled by still in plush terry bathrobes and slippers, accompanied by young aides holding their arms and guiding their steps.

As Lord Johnston approached, dirty white apron covering a dark shirt and navy work pants, Hudson reached out to him.

"Stick around, bro. We need to talk to you."

Johnston stopped and stood to one side of the tall detective. "Now?" he asked. "I'm busy. I've got lunch to prepare."

"We need just a moment of your time. Please wait until everyone's left."

Johnston leaned against the wall and assumed his usual frown.

When Stanley Cubbage walked by, still holding the greasy cloth with a pattern of stains that complimented the ones on his pants, Cortez reached out to him too.

"You" was all she said. Stanley didn't protest. He'd expected to be detained. After all, he had a record. He didn't know if the detectives knew about his record, but they certainly would find out when they punched his name into the computer at headquarters.

"Shay was a coworker," Hudson said to the two men after everyone else had left the room. "Either of you have a problem with her?"

"No, we rarely spoke," Johnston said first. He figured nothing would be gained by complaining about Shay's critiques of his food and his staff. He wasn't going to mention the argument between her and Rawley Bingham, Jr. either. *No business of mine. That's how you stay out of trouble, by not messing around in someone else's.*

"Not in passing? Not to discuss a resident?"

"No. All I do is cook. I put the meals on the table. I don't interact with anyone else but my staff." Johnston spoke softly, politely but stubbornly, nonetheless.

"And you?" Cortez asked nodding at Cubbage.

"She never came down to the basement," he said. "If she needed me to look at sum'in, like change a bulb or fix a spigot, she'd leave a note with Tess 'n Tess would put it in my mailbox."

Stanley wouldn't look Cortez in the eyes. He stared at the floor. He knew this made him look guilty, but he was. Guilty of being caught with a few marijuana cigarettes and a couple of hits of acid back when he was eighteen, just old enough to go to jail. Intent to sell, the cops had said. Cubbage knew it was bull at the time, but those were the days when young men were being sent to jail for possession of amounts that were now overlooked. It'd been his bad luck to be born at the wrong time.

"You both can go," said Cortez.

"We'll be back," Hudson added.

Johnston and Cubbage left together but soon parted without a word to the other. Johnston strode up to the kitchen, and Cubbage scuttled back to the basement.

Before leaving, Cortez and Hudson stopped to talk to Tess.

"Did you know the victim?" Cortez asked her.

"I didn't know her well," Tess said.

"How about friends? Did anyone come to see her here?"

"No, I never saw her hang out with anyone. She never mentioned any friends. We would occasionally chat about business stuff, you know, upcoming events and our jobs. That was all."

"Well, okay," Cortez sighed. "Here's my card. Let me know if anything happens or if anyone wants to talk to us."

"Will do," Tess promised.

"Now, who is the nurse on duty?" asked Cortez.

"Winnie Fields. She's in the infirmary on the third floor. Shall I call her?"

"Yes, please."

Winnie answered and told Tess, "Send the police up."

When the detectives arrived, they found an older woman of mixed background with her hair pulled back in a tight bun. Her figure was sturdy and her clothes tidy. She wore no make-up or jewelry.

Winnie was glad to show them the cabinet where the different controlled medications were housed. Atop the cabinet was a black notebook indicating which nurse had removed which drug, the amount taken, the name of the patient it was intended for, and the date. The last entry was at the bottom of a right-hand page for Saturday, October 27. The next page, Sunday, had been torn out.

"Who tore this out?" Hudson asked.

"I don't know." Winnie was suddenly flustered. "I hadn't looked at it yet today. I didn't realize a page was missing." She looked down and wrung her hands in her lap. "You have to believe me. I didn't steal any drugs. I don't know who did this."

"You'll need to do an inventory and see if anything is missing. Then come down to the station and make a statement," Cortez told her.

"I have to be here," she cried. "With Shay gone, there's no one to cover for me when I go to lunch."

"Then come down after work," Cortez said kindly.

"Yes, of course."

"And we'll need to take this notebook with us."

"I understand."

The detectives left.

"What do you think?" Hudson asked once they were out of earshot.

"I don't think she was lying," Cortez answered.

They took the elevator down to the lobby.

"Let's go," Cortez said to her partner.

Tess watched them leave and thought, *They'll be back.* Her stomach flip-flopped.

"Next stop, the husband, right?" Hudson said to Cortez, heading to their car.

They were five minutes from L'Automne to the residential sections bordering South Union Street. The Dinsmore home was a squat bungalow of fading white clapboard that needed a good power wash. A dirty green Saturn sat in the driveway. The detectives pulled in behind it.

The dirt on the siding and the sparse dying lawn gave the small home an air of sadness and neglect. There were no decorative bushes or fall flowers. Cortez had already formed an opinion of the man who cared so little for his lawn and car. Hudson rapped loudly on the faded black door.

The door opened a crack, and a man's face appeared. He had the sagging facial wrinkles and sad eyes of someone who found little joy in life.

"What do you want?" he asked.

"Do you have a few more minutes for us, Mr. Dinsmore?" Hudson asked.

"Yeah."

"We need to ask you some more questions about your wife."

"She's dead. You already know that."

"Yes, we do, and that's why we're here. It's a homicide, and we need to question everyone."

"I already spoke to your people this morning."

"We just have a few more questions," Hudson said. "May we come in?"

"Okay." The man stepped back, and the detectives could see that he was still in his bathrobe, a plaid wool wrap that looked as frayed and worn as its owner. He led them to the dining room and pointed at the chairs with his right hand.

"Have a seat. Would you like some coffee? There's some left in the pot." As he spoke, he pushed piles of old mail, store circulars, and dirty china cups to one side.

Cortez half-wondered if the coffee would taste like warm mud. "No, thank you," she said.

Hudson shook his head to indicate he didn't want any either.

The three sat down together, and Cortez pulled out her notebook.

"When was the last time you saw your wife?" she asked.

"At dinner last night. Then she went out. She said she was going to Walmart to buy Halloween decorations."

"And she didn't come home?"

"No, I guess not. I fell asleep on the sofa while watchin' the TV. Woke up this morning and saw she wasn't here."

"But you didn't call in a missing person's report?"

"Hell, no. She could have left for work, or sometimes, Shay stays out all night. She likes it there at that assisted living place. Says it's her family. They let her bunk down in an empty room. Or at least that's what she says."

"And you were at home all night?" Hudson asked.

"Yeah. Like I told ya. Asleep in front of the TV."

"Can anyone corroborate that?"

"Nope."

Cortez decided to ask the tough question. "You don't seem particularly upset at your wife's passing."

"Me and Shay was over. We have been for years. But we get along okay, so we decided it'd be better for the kids 'n all to stay livin' together. She was a good wife. But there was no spark left, if you know what I mean. She was a bit of a cold fish."

"You won't miss her?" Cortez asked.

"Oh yeah, I'll miss her. Especially her cookin'. But like I said, we wasn't much together."

"Do you work, Mr. Dinsmore?" Hudson asked.

"I do plumbing and a few other handyman-type jobs. I'm self-employed. I like it that way. Make my own hours."

"Did Shay have any enemies?" Cortez asked. "Anyone with a grudge?"

"Hell, half of Kennett hated her guts. She'd make up rumors about people she didn't like. Said the town manager was cooking the books. Said police were taking bribes, but you would know more about that than I would."

"I assure you, Mr. Dinsmore," Hudson broke in. "Our police officers don't take bribes."

"If you say so. But you go out and knock on any door in our neighborhood, and you'll hear how Shay claimed one teenage girl had an abortion, or Mr. So-and-so was cheating on his wife, or how the grocery store was repackaging old meat and putting new dates on it."

"Any truth in these allegations?"

"Who knows? I don't bother myself with it."

"Do you think any of these people would be angry enough to kill your wife?"

"I doubt it. No one has paid any attention to her for years. You get tired of hearing it and tune her out. That's what I do."

"Well, if you think of anything that might be helpful, please give us a call," Cortez said and handed him her card.

"We'll see ourselves out," Hudson said, and both detectives rose to leave.

Mr. Dinsmore stayed seated at the dining room table.

Once outside, Hudson said to Cortez, "Think he did it?"

"No, killing is hard work. He's too lazy."

CHAPTER THIRTEEN

Around eight that evening, after having a quiet dinner of spaghetti and canned fruit, Emily was finishing up in the kitchen when her phone rang.

"I was just talking to my mom," Bob said, his voice grave. "That Activities Coordinator we met at my mom's assisted living facility, Shay Dinsmore, was found murdered this morning."

"How terrible! How did she die?"

"Don't know. She was found in a dumpster behind the Walmart on Route 1. Didn't you see it on the news?"

"Haven't had time to watch tonight; I had bills to pay. Is your mom upset?"

"She's taking it okay. But there's quite a buzz around the facility. People are blaming Shay for things that have gone missing lately."

"That could include your mom's credit card."

"Exactly. Did I tell you that her friend Rawley's money clip disappeared then mysteriously reappeared in a bureau drawer minus the two hundred dollars cash that was in it? Shay probably got scared and put it back when he was out of his room. She had keys to everything."

"Do the police think someone at L'Automne killed her?"

"It's certainly a possibility."

"Are any of those seniors strong enough to kill someone? I'm sure she would have fought back."

"There's the staff," Bob suggested.

"I don't want to jump to any conclusions, but Lord Johnston is a powerful-looking man."

"There's a handyman also. I'm sure the police will talk to them. Are you free to visit my mom with me tomorrow after work?"

"No problem. Are you worried about your mom? Do you think she's safe?"

"I don't know. Shay Dinsmore was a local person. She could have lots of enemies outside of L'Automne."

"Is she married?"

"I don't know that either. Your questions are making me even more worried. Let's leave right after work tomorrow. Do you mind a late dinner?"

"Not at all. Let's hope we know more information tomorrow. Try to get some sleep. Give me a call when you're ready to leave."

"Will do. Love you."

That was a first. It took Emily a moment to recover from this quick declaration he rarely shared outside the bedroom.

"Love you too," she whispered back. "Good night."

When Rawley Bingham, Sr. heard about Shay Dinsmore's death, he had become concerned. Although he would miss the bothersome woman who only meant well, he was unnerved by her passing. He went to his desk and took out the folder of ledger pages Shay had left with him several days before.

"There's a problem with these figures," she had said. "I know you used to be an accountant. Maybe you can find it and tell me what to do."

When he had asked Shay where she had gotten the ledger pages, she had replied, "They're copies of L'Automne's income and expense reports for the past year. He's claiming much higher expenses than we actually have. I don't know a lot about the income, but I know we didn't spend thousands of dollars on arts and crafts supplies this year."

"What am I looking for?" Rawley had asked.

"Proof that he's embezzling," Shay said. "Then I'll report him to the board."

Now that Shay is dead, Rawley thought, *I'd better take a closer look at those pages. Could they have anything to do with her death? Maybe Catherine will find some proof that I haven't. And if she does, will that put us both in danger?*

Stanley Cubbage was in the basement laundry room scrubbing a stubborn stain from his hands. His white tee shirt was soaked in sweat. His brown work pants were covered in dirt and grease. He had been the handyman at L'Automne since it first opened in the 1980s. He knew every patched leak and blocked mouse hole in the building. He knew when residents used the toilet and when they were out of their rooms. He knew Lord Johnston snuck an occasional beer while at work and that Shay Dinsmore had been screwing the director, her sister's husband.

He also suspected that one of the nurses' aides occasionally stole pain meds for her boyfriend. Something was definitely fishy about Tess Tuesday too. He would get to the bottom of it. No one could keep a secret from him and his collection of room keys.

CHAPTER FOURTEEN
Tuesday, October 30

Before her demise, Shay had planned a host of Halloween activities for the residents of L'Automne. Most of those activities would not happen now, although Nichole Drago had offered to supervise Wednesday's Halloween party.

Nichole didn't know that Shay planned to use her own money to provide more Halloween decorations. Now, the items Shay had bought sat in her car in the police impound lot. Luckily, Shay had given Lord the money to buy pumpkins the week before.

After a quick meeting Monday evening, the service staff decided to continue with the pumpkin carving contest. Lord asked Nichole Drago to oversee the event. She was only too happy to oblige.

On Tuesday afternoon, after lunch was cleared, Nichole Drago stood up and addressed the room, "Shay planned this activity, and I think we should continue with it and with our party. She would want that. She cared about you all deeply. Now, please stay in your seats while the servers place newspapers, a pumpkin, carving instruments, and paints and brushes on each table. You have two hours to create the prettiest, scariest, or most imaginative pumpkins. Prizes will be awarded at four o'clock in the lounge. Drinks and snacks will also be served. Good luck!"

After she sat down, Harold took her hand and squeezed it. "Well done," he said.

Catherine and Rawley decided to paint Minnie and Mickey Mouse on their pumpkins. Across the table from them, Nichole and Harold were working on more typical jack-o'-lantern faces with clown-sized grins and round noses.

At four o'clock, the contestants and resident onlookers assembled in the lounge to hear whose pumpkins had been awarded prizes.

First prize was given to a couple Catherine didn't know well for elaborate pirate pumpkins resembling Captain Hook and Smee from Peter Pan. They had even taken their luncheon napkins and cleverly folded them to imitate a pirate hat for Hook and a bandanna for Smee. A surprised Mrs. Gunn won second prize for a pumpkin with a scary witch's face. Honorable mentions went to several other pleased contestants. Everyone clapped when Lord Johnston said the pumpkins would decorate the tables at the Halloween party.

As the workday wound down at Mirety Bank, Emily sat at her desk preparing her material for the next week's class. She was trying to forget the scrutiny she would be under. The new director and manager would be monitoring every class, reviewing the training manual, and even examining her email.

The phone rang. Emily was surprised to see that it was six o'clock.

"Ready?" Bob asked. "Meet you in the lobby in five." He hung up. No hello, no good-bye. He was worried, Emily knew. She was apprehensive herself and worried about Mrs. Bowie.

She shut down her computer, grabbed her coat and purse, and walked to the elevators. As she pressed the down button, the one to her left opened with a soft shush. She sighed as the door closed, and the elevator swiftly descended to the lobby. Her stomach flip-flopped with the sudden motion.

Exiting, she showed her ID badge to the new security guard who had been hired after the tragedy of 9/11. All the banks were still on high alert. Employees now had to show badges to security guards when both entering and leaving the building.

"You have a good evening, miss," he said.

"You too," Emily answered.

Another elevator whispered open and Bob emerged, frowning. After he showed his ID to the guard, he said to Emily, "Let's go."

"We should hurry before it gets too dark," Emily said. "You know what night this is."

"Not sure what you mean," Bob replied.

"That's right, you're not from around here," Emily said. "In Wilmington, the night before Halloween is called 'Mischief Night.' When I was young, you went out with your friends, a bar of soap, and some loose corn."

"To do what?" asked Bob as he and Emily hurried to the parking lot.

"Soap windows and throw corn at houses. At least that's what we did in the fifties and sixties. Somewhere along the line in the seventies, kids got more violent. They started throwing tomatoes and eggs at front doors and stole anything outside the house that wasn't nailed down. Homeowners would come rushing out of their houses with baseball bats to stop them. My brother used to sit outside his house with a garden hose to surprise anyone who dared come near. It got so violent in the late eighties that the mayor and governor declared Mischief Night was forbidden and imposed a curfew stating that everyone under eighteen had to be inside after 6 p.m. Things calmed down a lot after that, but every so often, a group of teenagers will decide to resurrect pre-curfew traditions. Did you do anything like this where you grew up in Pennsylvania?"

"Well, not in my neck of the woods. Although someone once recommended I read a book called *The Mischief Night Massacre*. I never got around to it though."

At Bob's SUV, Emily smiled as Bob graciously opened the passenger side door for her. As she started to get in, she noticed a scattering of white papers on the floor.

"Hold up," she said. "Let me pick up these papers that are on the floor. I don't want to step on them."

"Oh, sorry about that," Bob responded. "That's just some copies of accounting sheets my mother wanted me to look at. She faxed them to me yesterday. She thinks they have something to do with the director and Shay Dinsmore. She wants to know if I can find anything suspicious in them. I've no idea how she expects me to do that, but I told her I'd look at them."

Emily leaned down to pick up the papers and slid into the front seat.

"Do you mind if I look at them?" she asked. "I love number puzzles. I've gone through three or four books of them on the expert level."

"No way," Bob replied as he settled in the driver's side. "I thought you said you hated math in high school."

"I did. And, in college, I got a *D* in the easiest math course on campus. But that's because I couldn't do trig and calculus. I took an accounting class sponsored by the bank and got an *A*."

"So you can add and subtract, but that's it."

"Hey, I can divide and multiply too," Emily defended herself but laughed as she said it. "Seriously, I always use math in the grocery store to figure out the best buy. I can calculate the cost per ounce or per pound up to two decimal points. Just don't ask me to plot the trajectory of a rocket ship to the moon."

"Not to worry. I couldn't do that either."

As they traveled, Emily glanced at the papers. She tried to put them back in order. They looked like photocopies of ledger pages. She could see amounts paid out for salaries, amounts to the government for taxes, food costs, utility bills, and lots of miscellaneous purchases for decorations and events.

"There's something odd about these amounts," Emily said.

"What? Are the salaries out of line, or are they spending too much on food?" Bob asked.

"No, it's not that. It's the distribution of the numbers."

"What do you mean?"

"Like how many times a particular number appears in a list."

"What are you talking about? Why would it make a difference if, say, the number three appears fifty times and the number eight appears twenty times?"

"It does make a difference."

"You're kidding me, right?"

"No, there is a law about this. It's called Benford's Law for the guy who discovered it."

"Discovered what? Voodoo economics?"

"Now you're making fun of me again." She was getting a bit peeved at Bob for discounting her intelligence.

"No, no, I'm not. But I've never heard of Benford's Law. Is that like Murphy's Law where if anything can go wrong, it will? Or the Peter Principle—my personal favorite being in Human Resource— that says that people are promoted to their level of incompetence?"

"Not exactly. Benford's Law states that in any list of numbers, the leading digit of an entry is most often a small number."

"You mean there should be more entries beginning with a one or two rather than an eight or nine?"

"Yes, like that. I don't remember the explanation, or even if there is one. Anyway, I'm looking at lists of numbers where seven, eight, or nine appear in the first position more frequently than one, two, or three. That's suspicious."

"Suspicious of what?"

"That these numbers are bogus. Made up. Fudged. Whatever you want to call it."

"Where did you ever learn about Benford's Law? In your accounting class? I've taken two or three myself, and I don't remember any mention of that law."

"I saw it on a *Nova* program on PBS. Where did you say these papers came from?"

"Rawley Bingham gave them to my mom. Knowing she used to be a bookkeeper, he hoped Mom could tell him why Shay thought they were suspicious. He didn't see anything wrong with the numbers; my mom didn't either. So she sent me the papers to look at."

"Why did Shay think they were suspicious?"

"Rawley said Shay said they showed amounts for decorations, snack food, employee gifts, and even furniture that she knew were false. She wanted to prove it."

"Then whoever is writing checks for these amounts is embezzling money."

"That would be Weir. And Shay found out. And now Shay is dead."

"That's a problem," Emily said and looked out the window as if a solution might be in the fading light and long shadows.

"What are we going to do? Should we confront Weir first? Maybe he has receipts to back up some of these purchases. All laws have their exceptions."

"We'll need to talk to him."

"We don't have any authority to do this."

"No, but let's see what his reaction is."

Daylight Savings Time had ended the previous weekend, and the unaccustomed darkness of the early evening cast an eerie pall on Emily's feelings. As they traveled on Route 7, wisps of fog clouded Bob's headlights, and the streetlights shone dimly on the black macadam. Emily shivered. Her sweater was not enough to keep the chill off, and her stomach was uneasy. Was it hunger or a premonition of what the evening held?

The fog swirling around L'Automne did little to ease her fears. The vermilion curtains were closed, and no light shone through.

Emily sensed a threat in the deepening gloom gathering around the building. She missed her clairsentient friend, Melinda, who might have made some sense of her foreboding, and wished she were there.

CHAPTER FIFTEEN

Arriving at L'Automne, Bob parked and went around to open the door for Emily.

"I want to check on my mom before we speak to Weir," Bob said. "I'm worried about her."

"Will she be in the dining room?"

"Probably not. They eat early here, like four-thirty or five. She's probably back in her room."

"What do we do if Weir attacks us, either verbally or physically?" Emily asked as they walked up the path to the entrance.

"I'm not going to accuse him of anything right off the bat," Bob said. "I'll say that I'm concerned about the solvency of the facility where my mom lives. She paid a lot of money to buy that apartment she's in and pays six hundred dollars each month for food, medical, and security services. If Weir's embezzling and the place goes bust, she'll lose all that."

"And if he's insulted and takes a swing at you for questioning L'Automne's financial stability?"

"I'm bigger than he is, and I weigh more. I'm sure I can take him."

Famous last words, Emily thought. She had seen Weir. He looked stronger than Bob.

Before they entered the building, Emily said, "I'd like to chat with Lord Johnston while you're checking on your mom. The staff often knows more about what's going on in a place like this than the director. Maybe he can tell us something about your mother's missing credit card or Mr. Bingham's money clip."

"I'm not sure that's a good idea. He might take it as an accusation," Bob said.

"I promise I won't say anything to offend him. Why don't you go on up to see your mother, and I'll join you in a few moments? Then we can look for Weir."

"Okay." Bob nodded.

They signed themselves in, noting Tess had left for the day and a nurse's aide was filling in. Bob headed for the elevator. Emily went into the dining room and looked around. There was an empty buffet table at one end on the right-hand side of a kitchen door. To the left of the door was an empty salad bar station. In the center of the room was a long table with a dozen or so decorated pumpkins. Approaching the table, Emily could see that the pumpkins had been carved and painted to represent various characters, from witches and skeletons to pirates and werewolves. Some were excellent. Two in particular, a pair of pirates from Peter Pan, wore blue ribbons saying first prize. Other pumpkins also had ribbons; the residents had been busy that day.

Crossing the room, Emily heard laughter from the kitchen area. She pushed through the swinging kitchen door and saw Lord Johnston talking to a female staff member. The girl had straight blonde hair and an insolent tilt to her head. Emily noticed that they each had a cigarette in one hand and a can of beer in the other. On the wall behind them was a sign that said "NO smoking allowed in common areas. NO alcohol drinking by the staff at any time."

When Lord Johnston saw Emily, he dropped his cigarette on the floor and began to grind it out with his foot. He said with a hint of annoyance, "Did you want something? I'm finished for the day."

"Oh," Emily said, faking surprise, "I guess I opened the wrong door. I'm looking for Mrs. Bowie. She wasn't in her room." Emily figured that if Lord and the girl were drinking and smoking in the kitchen, there was no way they would know if Mrs. Bowie was in her room or not.

Lord glared at her. "And you thought she was hanging out here?"

"The Activities Room is around here somewhere, isn't it?" Emily asked, showing innocent bewilderment. In truth, she didn't know where the Activities Room was located. Lord's belligerent attitude, though, had convinced her to change her plan of asking about the money clip and the credit card.

"Go back out to the lobby and down the steps. The Activities Room is on the lower level," Johnston said.

Emily needed a new tactic.

"Don't you just love Old Milwaukee?" she suddenly said and pointed to the girl's can of beer. "It's so cheap and yet tastes as good as Miller Lite."

"Yeah, my boyfriend drinks it too," the girl said, taken in by the ruse. She took another swig. Johnston glared at Emily, not sure what her intent was.

"You're lucky," Emily said. "I never had a job where I could drink beer on my break." She smiled. "Mrs. Bowie told me about Shay. You don't have any ideas about what happened to her, do you? I mean, you all work together. Did she have enemies?"

"Shay wasn't exactly friendly with the kitchen help," Johnston said.

"Yeah, she could be a right snoot," said the girl.

"I don't think we can help you." Johnston glared at Emily.

"I should be going," Emily said. "Thanks for your help." She wouldn't learn anything useful here; she went to find Bob and his mom.

Emily took the steps to the second floor where Catherine Bowie had her apartment. She passed signs for the Nursing Care and Dementia Wing, which was in the opposite direction from Catherine's apartment in the Assisted Living Wing.

Bob had told her that his mom had bought her apartment there while she could still care for herself and afford L'Automne's prices. However, being eighty-five, Catherine knew her days of independent living were few. L'Automne was a continuing care community, supporting independent to assisted to end-of-life care. She was uncomfortable with the idea of her son seeing her helpless. It was a matter of personal pride. She couldn't bear to have him change her diapers if it ever came to that.

Emily knocked softly on Catherine's door. She could hear anxious voices inside. When no one answered, she knocked louder.

Bob opened the door and was temporarily startled to see Emily. "It's you," he managed. "Come in. My mom is rather upset at the moment. She can't get a hold of her friend Rawley. He was at dinner and said he would come by to watch TV with her, but he hasn't shown up and is not answering his phone."

He stepped back and let Emily enter the apartment.

"Rawley Bingham, right?" Emily asked. "I've met him. I dated his son many years ago in high school."

"That sounds right," Catherine replied. "His son is married now and has two children, I believe."

"Shall we go knock on Mr. Bingham's door?" Emily suggested.

They left the apartment, and Catherine led them past seven or eight other apartments, stopping at the last door on the right, Number 221. Catherine knocked, but no one answered.

She knocked again and called out, "Rawley?"

CHAPTER SIXTEEN

Rawley didn't answer. Catherine tried the knob and found it unlocked. Cautiously she began to open the door, but it was blocked by something on the other side.

"Son, help me," she said.

Emily thought she heard a door slam somewhere inside the apartment but decided they should focus on getting inside first.

Bob pushed heavily against the door. When he got it open a few inches, he could see—what he had hoped not to see—the back of Rawley's bald head and his body on the entryway floor. The way he was lying blocked the door.

"Let's push," Bob said to Emily. "We have to see if he's hurt."

Working together, they continued pushing the door until they had moved him enough to get inside. Rawley was sprawled lifelessly between the door and the kitchen. Bob and Emily stepped around him and simultaneously knelt, one on either side of him. They saw a hypodermic needle with fluid in it lying next to Mr. Bingham's head.

"I think we interrupted someone," Emily said, noticing a red mark on Rawley's neck.

Pointing to the needle, she added, "Don't touch that. It's evidence."

"Oh, Rawley, what happened to you," Catherine cried and started to kneel by his head.

"Find a phone and call 911 for an ambulance," Bob gently said to her, and Catherine ran to the phone.

Bob put his ear to Rawley's mouth to check for a breath, then shook his head. "No breath."

"I know CPR," Emily said, although she hadn't used it since she tried reviving her friend Rosie in 1995. She had been unsuccessful then. She prayed for a better result this time.

Emily checked for a pulse in the carotid artery. None. Next, she put her finger in Rawley's mouth; Bob guessed this was done to ensure Rawley hadn't swallowed his tongue. Emily bent down and blew air into Rawley's mouth. Rawley's chest was unresponsive.

"You count," she said to Bob and positioned her arms to do chest compressions.

"Okay," he said, hearing his mother talking to 911 and mentally berating himself for being so slow to act.

Emily started CPR, and Bob counted: one, pause; two, pause; three, pause. At four, he looked again at the red mark—like a mosquito bite—on Rawley's neck. At seven, he decided he wouldn't mention this to his mother. By the count of ten, he was sure Rawley had been murdered.

As Emily continued CPR, Bob heard his mother at the apartment door calling down the hallway, "Nurse! Is there a nurse anywhere on the floor?"

Catherine wasn't sure what to do now, so she silently knelt behind Emily and watched her try to save Rawley's life.

Suddenly, from the kitchen behind Bob, a nurse appeared. She was short but strong-looking, with well-defined arms and an anxious look on her face.

"Where did you come from?" Emily asked her.

"The back stairs. There's an entrance in this kitchen. I was in the nurse's station right above us on the third floor, heard the commotion, and ran down. Let me take over for you."

"No, I'm fine. I've had training in CPR. Why don't you meet the EMTs?" As she said this, they heard the approaching wail of an ambulance. Looking dubious, Winnie Fields went out into the corridor.

Bob continued his counting; they were somewhere in the nineties by now.

The siren grew louder and stopped outside the front door of the building. It seemed like only seconds before two EMTs and a stretcher were through the door and filling up the room.

Gratefully, Emily got up and let the EMTs take over. Bob gingerly stepped back from Rawley's still unresponsive body.

As one EMT began to apply pressure, Rawley's body jerked, and he took a sharp breath. The EMT stopped and knelt back on his heels. Rawley took another breath and opened his eyes. Feelings of relief flooded the room.

"Thank God," Catherine murmured. "Rawley, who did this to you?"

He shook his head back and forth but didn't speak.

"Leave him alone for now," the EMT said. "He's too weak to talk. Do any of you know what happened?"

Emily pointed to the needle where they had left it on the floor. "You'll want to take that," she said. "I'm guessing the attacker tried to inject a drug into Mr. Bingham's neck." She pointed out the red mark.

The EMT picked up the needle and deposited it in a clear plastic bag.

"Thanks for not touching that," he said.

"Let's sit down," Emily suggested to the others.

Bob, Emily, Catherine, and Winnie went into the living area while the EMTs stabilized Rawley and prepared to move him.

"I'll go to the hospital with him and call you later," Winnie Fields told Catherine. The EMTs were now putting Rawley on a stretcher to wheel him out. Winnie rose to join them.

"You did a great job," one EMT said to Emily; his name tag read "Jimmy."

"I'm very thankful he came around, Jimmy." Emily smiled.

"Tell Rawley we love him," Catherine said to Jimmy as he and Elijah took the stretcher away.

"Of course," Jimmy said.

Once they were gone, Catherine sat on the sofa and cried. Her sobs were as quiet and controlled as was the rest of her but heart-wrenching nonetheless.

Emily went to the kitchen to get her a glass of water. As she drew near the sink, her foot kicked something that skittered across the floor. She looked down and saw a blue Bic lighter.

She picked it up and brought it into the sitting room with the glass of water.

"Mrs. Bowie, please try to drink a little water."

"Thank you, dear," she said, raising her head and taking the glass. She took a sip and sighed. "I'll be okay," she said.

Emily held up the blue lighter. "Is this Mr. Bingham's?" she asked.

"Why, no, dear," Catherine said. "Rawley doesn't smoke."

"He might have one to have around, maybe to light candles with?" Emily suggested.

"Well, if he did, I never saw it before," Catherine responded.

Someone rapped on the open door. They all looked up to see a nurse's aide with a woman.

"That's Detective Cortez," Catherine said. "She came here the day Shay was killed."

"Sorry to bother you folks," Cortez said, "but the police always follow up a 911 call. You might remember me. I'm Detective Cortez. I've spoken to the EMTs. They said Mr. Bingham was perhaps assaulted. They mentioned a red mark on his neck, possibly from a needle that was found."

Hearing this, Catherine broke into fresh sobs. Bob moved closer to her and put his arm around her.

Catherine raised a tear-stained face. "Assaulted? Why? Who would want to hurt that poor, dear man?"

Cortez took out a small black notebook and began to write in it. She replied, "You need to tell *me*, ma'am. Was he fighting with anyone here at L'Automne? Had anyone threatened him recently?"

Catherine looked to Bob and Emily as if they might know better than she. Bob shook his head silently. He wasn't sure if he should bring up the ledger pages, but since his mom didn't mention it, he decided he shouldn't either.

"No one," Catherine finally said. "Everybody loves Rawley."

"And where were all of you at the time of the alleged assault?" Cortez asked.

"I was in my room waiting for my son," Catherine replied.

"Emily and I came to see my mother," Bob explained. "We had just arrived; you can check the sign-in log. My mother said she couldn't get Mr. Bingham on the phone, so we decided to go to his room. That's when we found him."

Emily nodded in agreement. She didn't see her visit to the kitchen as being relevant to Rawley's attack.

"Did you see anyone leaving the room or in the hallway?" Cortez asked.

"No," Bob replied.

"I thought I heard a door close right when we knocked on Mr. Bingham's door," Emily offered. "But I didn't see anyone else in the apartment."

"There's a door to the back stairs in Rawley's kitchen," Catherine said. "But I don't remember hearing a door close."

"I didn't either," Bob added. "But we could have been too distracted by trying to push the door open."

"I'm sure it's too late now to investigate those stairs," Cortez sighed. "But I will have an officer follow up on it tomorrow. Are you aware of any connection between Mr. Bingham and the deceased Mrs. Dinsmore?" She directed this question to Catherine.

"No. I mean, Shay was the Activities Coordinator, but she didn't have any other sort of relationship with Rawley. They were friendly, but Shay was friends with everyone." It didn't cross Catherine's mind to mention the ledger pages Rawley had given her. Bob and Emily noticed this omission and chose to follow Catherine's lead.

"Thank you." Cortez snapped her notebook shut.

"Ms. Cortez," Emily said. "I found this lighter in the kitchen. It might have been left by the person who attacked Mr. Bingham."

Cortez pulled a small plastic bag from her purse, reached out her hand, and took the lighter. She deposited it in the bag.

"Do you know who this belongs to?" she asked, looking at each one.

All shook their heads.

"Thank you. I'll be back in the morning to question the director, staff, and residents." She gave Bob and Catherine her card. "Call me if you think of anything."

She reached down and touched Catherine on the shoulder. Her face relaxed into a softer expression. "I'm so sorry your friend was attacked. Please don't hesitate to call me if you think of something else or feel threatened in any way." She straightened up, nodded to them, and said, "Good night." Then she left.

"Come home and stay with me tonight, Mom. I'm worried about your staying here."

"Nonsense, I'll be fine. Rawley will recover. And I need to be here to comfort our friends tomorrow."

Bob was torn. His mom seemed to be dismissing the fact that Rawley was attacked.

"Please, Mom. I won't be able to sleep worrying about you."

"I'll call you first thing in the morning. I promise," she said. "Now I want to go to bed."

Grudgingly, he acceded to Catherine's wishes. Perhaps he had been wrong about the mark on Rawley's neck. If the hospital determined it resulted from the assault, the hospital would notify the police.

"Yes, call me first thing in the morning," he told her.

"I promise. Now let's go back to my apartment. I'm too tired to do anything else this evening. I'll be okay."

Bob said, "We'll walk you back."

Little was said as Bob and Emily accompanied Catherine to her apartment. Bob kissed her tenderly on the cheek and said, "We'll talk tomorrow."

Catherine, with a sad smile, nodded and shut the door behind them.

"What a horrible experience for your mom," Emily said as they started downstairs.

Bob answered, "And I can't believe you never told me you know CPR. You were like an angel sent from heaven."

"No, I wasn't," Emily contradicted him. "But thank goodness it worked."

When they got to the reception desk, they asked the nurse's aide sitting there if the director was in his office.

"I'm afraid he's gone for the day," she said. "But what happened to Mr. Bingham? I saw the EMTs with him."

"We don't know," Emily said.

"I'll be back tomorrow," Bob said, and Emily hoped that would be soon enough.

CHAPTER SEVENTEEN

"You hungry?" Bob asked as they walked to his car. "We can stop somewhere for food."

"No, I'm too exhausted," Emily said. "I'm ready to crawl into bed with a good book. But do you think your mom is safe?"

"I couldn't convince her to stay with me, but I'd like to go back tomorrow morning. I still want to ask Weir about those ledger pages. I'll take a sick day. You want to join me?"

"Yes, I do, and I don't have a training class right now, but what will my new bosses think if I call in sick two days after they've arrived? And who do I even call tomorrow morning? I don't have their names or phone numbers."

"The director is Felicia Fyk, and make sure you say it to sound like 'ick.'"

"I get it."

"And the new manager is Lark Pettet. But as for calling in sick tomorrow, call John Balboa like you would have done last week. He'll pass on the news when he sees them."

"This isn't going to look good to them."

"I've got your back," Bob said. "You are allowed a certain number of sick days."

"Okay, I will. I'm concerned about your mom too."

"I saw that red mark on Rawley's neck. And what about the needle?" Bob suddenly said. "I'm worried that someone tried to kill him."

"Well, I guess we can count Lord Johnston out," Emily said. "I saw him drinking beer and smoking cigarettes with one of his staff. How about Weir? Did you see him anywhere when you went to your mom's apartment?"

"No," Bob said, "But not seeing him doesn't prove he had or hadn't left."

"What about the maintenance man?"

"I didn't see him either. It's late evening. I'd expect him to have left already."

"Either one could have used those back stairs into Rawley's apartment."

"Right. Well, it could be anybody. Thank goodness my mom has nothing like that in her apartment."

They rode in silence for a while, each consumed by their thoughts. When they got to Emily's house, it was 10 p.m.

"I'm beat," Emily said as she got out. "Call me in the morning and let me know what you want to do."

"It'll be Halloween," Bob said. "Who knows what might happen?"

"Thanks for that cheery thought. See you tomorrow."

Emily let herself in the house, fed Zoe her dinner, and munched on a few Triscuits for her own meal. She swallowed them down with a glass of Pinot Grigio. Before she had a chance to worry about Mrs. Bowie, she was fast asleep.

CHAPTER EIGHTEEN
WEDNESDAY, OCTOBER 31

Emily hated calling in sick, especially when she wasn't ill. She was proud of the years she had taken no sick days. Now, with a new Training Director and Training Manager, she was possibly starting off her relationship with them on the wrong foot. Their first day in the office, and she would be absent.

At eight on the dot Wednesday morning, Emily called John Balboa's office number. He didn't answer, so she left a message on his machine. In fact, she was relieved that he didn't answer. He would have pointed out her career faux pas.

Tess greeted Bob and Emily at the front desk when they arrived at L'Automne. "Good morning! Your mom must be thrilled to be seeing so much of you."

"I'm a little concerned because of everything that's been happening around here," Bob said.

Tess grimaced but quickly regained her smile. "Don't you worry about a thing," she said. "I'm sure nothing else will happen. The director and I are hyperaware of everything that goes on."

"I only want my mom to be safe."

"She is. Please don't be concerned."

"Is the director in yet?" Bob asked.

"He is. The police are with him. You can go on up and wait," Tess told them.

After they signed themselves in, Emily asked Bob, "Do you think we should stop by your mom's first and let her know we're here?"

"No. I don't want to miss Weir again."

As they crossed the lobby and climbed to the office, they met Detectives Cortez and Hudson coming down the stairs. The grim-faced detectives nodded to them but kept going.

The door was open, so Bob didn't bother to knock. Weir was sitting at his desk holding a small mirror in his hand. He was looking into the mirror and smoothing his hair to cover his receding hairline. He was startled to see them.

"What do you want?" he asked grumpily, hastily putting the mirror in a drawer. "I have enough problems already."

"Sorry," said Bob, in a tone that didn't indicate regret. "Emily and I have some questions for you."

Bob started to sit in one of the chairs across the desk from Weir, but Weir held his hand up to indicate that he should stop. "Don't bother sitting down. I'm on my way out. Can you come back another day?"

"No." Emily set the papers that were in her hand on the desk. "I've been looking at your ledger numbers. They're incorrect."

"Who are you, and why would you think that?" Weir asked, shifting in his chair nervously.

Bob and Emily stood there, staring at him, letting him squirm. Weir stayed silent, thinking fast.

After a moment, Emily continued, "I'm a friend of Bob's, and someone gave us a few pages of your expense accounts ledger. I've been examining them. I don't think they're accurate. The numbers don't make sense," Emily said, trying to be nonconfrontational but not succeeding.

"We want to know if this business is solvent or not," Bob added.

"Of course it's solvent! How would you know what my ledger entries should be? How dare you stand there and accuse me of incompetence."

"Emily..." Bob started to say, but Emily shook her head. She didn't want to show their hand. If Weir knew how they knew, he could redo the numbers.

"What would you say to my handing them over to the police?" Emily asked.

"For what reason?" Weir demanded. "I've done nothing wrong. There's no evidence to suggest I've committed a crime. They won't do anything."

"So my mother is safe here?" Bob interjected. "And her investment is safe here? You can guarantee that L'Automne is in the black?"

"Of course I can!" Weir said, struggling to appear calm, though mildly outraged at Bob's accusations. "Don't worry about your mother. This facility is running smoothly, and she has a home with us for as long as she wants. Where did you get your accounting information?"

"I'd rather not say," Emily replied.

"Then how do you know it's not accurate?"

"I trust my source," Bob said. "I'm going to hold onto these, so know that I'm concerned and will be paying close attention to my mother's monthly bills and any financial information she receives in the newsletter. I'll be looking at the previous month's income and expense report."

"Feel free to question me about any particular item," Weir said. "Now, if you don't mind, I have another appointment and must leave."

Bob picked the ledger pages up. He and Emily left the office. They didn't speak to avoid Weir overhearing them. When they reached the lobby, they quickly went up to Catherine's apartment.

Irritated, Weir left his office to speak to Tess. The lobby was empty; they had privacy. Their conversation wouldn't be overheard.

"I need to speak to you," Weir began.

"What do you want?" Tess asked quietly.

"Stanley Cubbage paid me a visit the other day."

"The maintenance guy?"

"Yes. He seems to doubt that you are who you say you are."

"Really? Why would he think that?"

"He said you weren't aware he'd previously tightened some screws on your wheelchair."

"I guess I forgot."

"Well, I'm not sure. Sometimes you do seem different."

"Different how?"

"That you're not Tess."

"I'm Tess. You have it all wrong. Stanley gets high down there in the basement. I wouldn't trust any judgments on his part." Tess paused, thinking quickly how to handle Weir. "The only thing that might have changed is my attitude," she said, looking him in the eyes with a soft flutter of lashes. "I've noticed what you've done here at L'Automne. The residents and staff don't seem to appreciate the improvements you've made. But I'm guessing what I think isn't important to you anymore. You used to care about what I thought." She hung her blonde head demurely and pretended to study her hands in her lap.

Weir looked at her closely. *What is she saying? Is she coming on to me?* Weir and Tess had had a brief fling when she was first hired, before her illness struck, but once she was disabled, he no longer found her attractive.

"I don't know what to say, Tess. You're a beautiful woman. It's a damned shame you've been cursed with this illness."

Tess looked up at him and smiled. "It doesn't keep me from doing most of what I want to do."

Weir was not buying her act. Suddenly he came around the desk to where she was sitting. He grabbed the arm rails and turned the wheelchair to face him.

"Did you send someone to snoop in my office? Did you copy pages out of my ledger? Did you give them to anybody?"

"Don't be ridiculous," Tess said. "My wheelchair doesn't climb stairs."

"This chair?" Weir said, moving behind her and grabbing the handles of her wheelchair.

"What are you doing? Let go of my chair!" This wasn't the outcome she'd expected.

Weir didn't say a word but pushed her toward the stairs down to the lower level. Tess was terrified he was going to push the wheelchair, and her, down the steps.

Before they reached the steps, Tess pulled on the chair's hand brakes. Weir fell forward on top of her, causing the chair to fall to one side and dumping them on the floor. Tess screamed as she fell.

Hearing the commotion, Lord Johnston ran out of the kitchen and found Tess and Weir on the floor near the top of the stairs.

"Are you okay?" he asked as they both started to sit up. He saw no blood on them or the floor, so he righted the wheelchair and helped Tess back into it. "What the bloody hell is going on here?" he asked.

Weir stood up, smoothed out his shirt, and walked away without a word.

"Thank you, Lord," Tess said. "I think I'll go home now and rest before the party."

"I'll forget what I just saw," Lord said, heading back to the kitchen. "That should even out some of the things I hope you'll forget about me."

"Of course." Tess smiled, her composure regained. *What things are Lord referring to that I can forget? And what is Weir talking about anyway? Ledger entries? His office is one area he knows I can't explore.*

Back at her desk, she called a nurse's aide. "Can you take over for me out front? I'm not feeling well. I need to go home."

The aide agreed and Tess set the phone to forward calls to the answering machine until the aide arrived. She got her purse and struggled into her coat. It was a short thick coat of camel hair's wool with a fake mink collar. Tess thought it looked glamorous next to her pale blonde hair. Very posh, like Marilyn Monroe.

She spun the wheels of her chair out from behind the desk and across the lobby to the elevator. Once safely inside, she descended to the lower level, where she could quickly exit to the parking lot.

When the elevator doors opened with a soft shushing sound, Tess forced the wheelchair over the tread where the elevator met the floor and onto the hallway's linoleum, trying to pick up speed. She was pleased with how muscular her arms had become using the wheelchair. Looking up, she suddenly pulled on the brakes and stopped. Shay stood not six feet from her in the middle of the hallway. Her brown hair was as disheveled as ever, and her face was milk-white. Her brown eyes were dark and intense, demanding attention. Tess was terrified; she began to shake. Shay was dead. Who was this?

In a shivery whisper, the figure exhaled, "I know who you are." Tess's arm and neck hair rose with an electric tingle.

"Who are *you*?" Tess demanded. She was surprised she could speak, given the tightness in her throat and chest.

"You know who I am," the figure replied.

"Shay? But you're dead!"

"I'm just on the other side, watching."

Tess began to wheeze; she felt her windpipe was about to close up.

"Your sister, I know your sister," the figure said and began to fade from view.

Tess watched in horror as little pieces of the apparition—for that was what it had to be—began to disappear. First, the arms, then the legs. The torso was next. Shay's chalky face hung in midair for a half second.

"I know your sister," Shay breathed again, the face breaking up: the forehead going first, then the cheeks, then the mouth and chin. Two brown eyes with a golden gleam hung in the air then vanished.

Tess felt nauseous. *I've seen a ghost. A ghost! What does that ghost know?*

CHAPTER NINETEEN

After leaving Weir's office, Bob and Emily went to Catherine's apartment.

"How are you, mom?" Bob asked before saying hello.

After kissing her son and smiling at Emily, Mrs. Bowie said, "As you can see, I'm fine."

"How's Rawley?" Emily asked.

"I talked to Rawley. He was stabbed with the needle. It had morphine, but he didn't get enough to kill him. The doctors wanted to keep him under observation last night. They're letting him come home later today. His son will stay with him tonight."

"But where did the attacker come from?" Catherine asked. "We were in the hallway."

"The back stairs," Emily said. "Don't you remember the nurse said that's how she got there? The attacker must have heard us and fled down those stairs. When you began pushing Rawley's door open, I thought I heard a door slam. That must have been the attacker making his escape."

"Now I remember. Yes, the back stairs into the kitchen."

"Do you know where else they lead?" she asked Catherine.

"Down to the lower level and the basement. I think there are back stairs in the North and South Wings. They're fire exits, and they're also used by maintenance personnel. The director doesn't like visitors to see cleaners and plumbers traipsing through the lobby."

"But it seems odd they can be accessed through a resident's kitchen," Emily said.

"This building was a private residence before it became a senior living facility," Catherine explained. "Perhaps Rawley's kitchen used to be a hallway before the building was redesigned for individual apartments."

"Makes sense." Emily nodded.

"I want to speak to the maintenance guy," Bob said. "Maybe he knows more than he's told the police. I bet he sees a lot of what goes on here."

"Good idea," Emily agreed.

"I'm going to lie down," Catherine said. "I'm tired. Come by when you're done talking to Stanley." She didn't add that she did not think Stanley was the one who stole Rawley's money or assaulted him. He was an obvious suspect; he had a key to everyone's room. And because he was so obvious, she doubted he was the culprit. "I want to hear about everything he says."

"Will do," Bob said.

CHAPTER TWENTY

"Before we see the maintenance guy, let's see if Rawley Bingham's apartment is open," Emily suggested. "We can try going down those back stairs and see where they lead."

Bob kissed his mom, and he and Emily continued down the hall to Room 221. Emily could see that, ideally, this area should have been left open for easy access to the fire exit. However, the builders probably decided to squeeze in one more apartment and put the exit in the kitchen.

They looked around to see if anyone was watching them, but the hallway was empty. Yellow police tape hung in strips on either side of the doorway, indicating that someone had already broken the seal. Bob tried the doorknob and found it was unlocked. He slowly opened the door. Seeing no one, he and Emily tiptoed in. They started for the kitchen.

"Hey!" shouted the man standing at the sink with a glass of water. "What are you doing in here?"

It was Rawley Bingham, Jr. Emily's heart dropped. What would he think of her now that she was breaking into his father's apartment?

"So sorry," Bob said. "We were looking for the back stairs."

Rawley Jr. blinked and silently considered the two.

Would he be angry and ask them to leave? Emily held her breath.

"They're right here," he said and pointed to a steel door at the end of the small galley kitchen. He decided not to be upset with them about sneaking into his father's apartment. He might need their help finding out who had attacked his father. The more eyes on a problem, the better, he figured.

"Why aren't you using the elevator?" he asked.

"We're trying to find out who attacked your father," Emily hastily explained. "This might be how he got in. We're also worried about Bob's mom. Whether or not she's safe here."

"And you think that person snuck in, attacked my father, and then escaped down the back stairs? But what I can't figure out is why. Oh, by the way, Emily, I need to thank you for giving my father CPR. I'm really grateful. He might have died." He smiled at her sadly.

Emily sighed inwardly with relief; it would be okay. Rawley wasn't mad at her anymore. She knew, though, that no apology would ever erase the hurt she had inflicted on a teenaged Rawley. "I was glad I was there to help," she said.

"I do not understand why anyone would want to hurt my father," Rawley said again, putting his empty glass in the sink. He turned toward the steel fire door and opened it. He checked out the concrete landing and walked over to the metal railings, looking up and down at the concrete stairs. Bob and Emily followed him. No one was on the stairs. All was quiet. They came back into the kitchen.

"Please sit down for a minute," Rawley said. "I came here to make sure everything was in place for my father's coming home later today."

They all found a chair in the tiny sitting room dominated by a thirty-five-inch TV.

"So," Rawley continued, "you never answered my question. Why do you think anyone would want to hurt my father?"

"I think it has to do with some ledger pages," Emily began. "Did your father show them to you?"

"No, he hasn't mentioned any ledger pages."

"Shay Dinsmore thought the director was embezzling money because the ledger sheets showed amounts for expenses that were not what she thought they should be. She made copies of them and gave them to your father because she knew he used to be an accountant. She thought he could figure out what was wrong with them."

"And then Shay was killed," Rawley said thoughtfully. "And my father was attacked."

"Yes," said Emily. "Now we're concerned about Bob's mom because your father gave *her* a copy of the ledger pages."

"Oh my," Rawley said, shaking his head and looking worried. "Do you have a copy of those pages? Could I see them?"

Emily took them from her purse and handed them to Rawley. The room was quiet except for the rustling of the ledger pages as Rawley examined them.

"I can't say I understand what's wrong with them just by looking at them," he said. "They all look like legitimate expenses."

"It's Benford's Law," Emily explained. "In any list of numbers, the majority should begin with a lower number, with the rest starting with a higher number. If you look at those ledger entries, most begin with an eight or a nine."

"I'm not sure that would hold up in a court of law," Rawley said. He reexamined the pages. "But I see that what you're saying is right. These entries begin with a high number rather than a two, three, or four. Seeing that a woman was killed and my father attacked, it's, at least, something to investigate. Turning to Bob, he asked, "How is your mom holding up?" Rawley wanted to change the subject until he had more time to consider Benford's Law.

"My mom refuses to come stay with me," Bob said. "Do you think your father is safe to come back here?"

"I've taken care of that," Rawley said, flashing a grim smile. "I'm an attorney, and one of my clients is a security firm. I've asked them to post a guard just inside my dad's door. That way the guard can hear if anyone tries to get in or comes in from the back stairs. I can include your mother's room tonight, and every night, until this is resolved."

"Shouldn't we ask the police to do that?" Bob asked.

"I doubt they have the extra manpower," Rawley replied.

"Thank you," Emily said and smiled. "We'd appreciate that so much."

"Do you think the director will object to your bringing in outside personnel?" Bob asked.

"Let him. Like I said, I'm an attorney. I can deal with the director. His facility is obviously unsafe. Can I have your phone numbers in case I have something to report to you? Here's my card if you need to call me."

Bob and Emily gave him their numbers and rose to leave.

"Thanks again," Bob said, and they left.

"I'm uncomfortable going back through Rawley's apartment to check out the back stairs," Emily said. "Let's take the elevator to the basement."

"Sounds good. Let's hope we can get some information from Stanley Cubbage."

CHAPTER TWENTY-ONE

Bob and Emily passed Catherine's door without stopping and took the elevator down to the basement. As the door opened, they were treated to that damp earth smell so many old basements exhale. Although the floor around the elevator was concrete, one had to wonder if there were areas in old storage rooms where the floor was still packed dirt.

They followed a hallway dimly lit with bare bulbs every ten feet, until they came to a brighter area with bulky tables. The walls were covered with pegboards holding screwdrivers, hammers, and other tools. There were also shelves containing drills and pieces of pipe. The air was damp and chilly. Emily shivered as she looked around. With a start, she discovered the disheveled maintenance man sitting quietly on a stool at a far table, silently observing them.

Emily nudged Bob, tilted her head at Stanley, and said, "Mr. Cubbage, hello. Do you have a minute to speak to us?"

Cubbage ignored her and looked directly at Bob. "You're Catherine Bowie's boy, ain't ya?" He set down the piece of machinery he was holding and turned his attention to them fully. "What do you need me fer?"

"Yes, I am. And this is my girlfriend, Emily. Sorry to disturb you. We'd like to ask you a question or two."

"Police have already done that."

"We know, but we'd feel better if we talked to you too."

"Fire away." Cubbage put a grease-stained hand into an equally grease-stained pocket. He pulled out a pack of cigarettes, took one out, put the pack away, and picked up matches.

"Are you allowed to smoke down here?" Bob asked.

"I make the rules down here," Cubbage answered, then lit his cigarette. He settled back on his stool, leisurely leaning against the worktable. "Now what's that question you got?"

Emily started. "We know that, doing maintenance, you see a lot of what goes on here. You probably don't attract attention when you walk around, and maybe you see or overhear things that others aren't aware of. We were hoping you could give us some insight into Shay Dinsmore and why you think she might have been killed."

"Shay?" Stanley sighed. "She was a good'un. You might not think it to talk to her at first, but she really did care about the residents here. I bin here quite a while. I never seen her do anything shady."

"Nothing to do with the director?" Emily pressed.

"Oh, that. A little wham-bam-thank-you-ma'am on the side? I don't have no problem with that. You gotta get it where you can is what I say." He took a long drag on his cigarette.

Emily didn't approve of what he meant, but she let it slide.

"Nothing else?" Bob asked. "Who do *you* think killed her?"

"Oh, I couldn't tell you that. I've got no proof. And who knows, I might be next. No, you'll get nothin' outta me about that."

"Sorry to have bothered you," Emily said, feeling defeated. She had felt sure he would have some information for them, some tidbit only a maintenance man might have discovered.

They turned to leave, and suddenly Stanley said, "Hey, I ain't done talkin' to ya." They turned around.

"You take a look at that crippled girl. Summin' ain't right about her."

"Like what?" Emily asked.

"Well, agin, I ain't sayin'. You'll have to figure it out for yurselves. I'm done now. You can leave." He waved his cigarette at them, indicating they should turn around and leave his personal space.

They did as told and walked back to the elevator.

"Well, that wasn't very helpful," said Bob as he pressed the elevator button. "I think we wasted our time."

"I disagree," said Emily. "Let's go talk to Tess."

CHAPTER TWENTY-TWO

When Bob and Emily returned to the lobby, they found a nurse's aide sitting behind the desk.

"Where's Tess?" asked Bob.

"She took a few hours off," the aide explained. "She should be back tonight for the party. Can I help you with anything?"

"No, thanks anyway," Bob said and turned to Emily.

"Shall we take my mom to lunch?"

"Yes, let's," she replied.

"Don't forget we have a Halloween party scheduled to begin at four-thirty this afternoon," the nurse's aide spoke up. "Remind Mrs. Bowie to wear her costume."

"Will do," Bob replied.

As they headed for the elevator, they could see the kitchen staff setting up the dining room with Halloween-themed paper tablecloths, napkins, plates, and cups. A carved pumpkin from the previous day's contest adorned each table. A few black and orange streamers were draped along the walls, but on the whole, the Halloween decorations looked pretty drab.

"I wonder if Shay had plans for nicer decorations," Emily mused as they waited for the elevator. Hadn't that been one of the ledger entries?

"If she did, they're probably impounded with her car at the police station."

"As I recall, over seven thousand dollars for decorations were mentioned in the account ledger. I only see about thirty dollars' worth in the dining room."

"Maybe that amount includes food for the party this afternoon or expenses for Thanksgiving and Christmas."

They rode in silence to the second floor and walked quietly to Catherine's apartment. Bob knocked softly on the door. His mother opened it immediately.

After greeting them, Catherine asked, "Was Stanley any help?"

"Afraid not," Bob replied. He chose not to share Stanley's thoughts on Tess. He couldn't see that being helpful.

"Do you need anything?" he asked.

"You can take me to lunch." she replied.

"Of course! That's why we're here," Bob said, happy to hear her ask.

"I want to go someplace really different today. I'm feeling a little bit wild and crazy. Maybe it's seeing what happened to Rawley, but I want to go somewhere I've never been before. Guess where!" She grinned, and a dimple appeared. Her blue eyes sparkled. Now that she knew Rawley would be okay, she could stop worrying.

"Where could that be?" Bob asked, smiling at his mom's good mood.

"I want to go to a casino. I want to gamble. I want to use the—what do they call them?—the one-armed bandits!"

Emily laughed out loud. She couldn't help herself. What a delightful woman Bob's mother was.

Bob was also surprised. *Mom—gambling? Rawley's attack must have really frightened her into thinking she could die tomorrow.* "Of course, but I'm not sure I know where to go. I think there's one somewhere around Philadelphia, but I've never been there."

"Oh, I thought you would know." Catherine's good spirits were instantly deflated. "I see them advertised on TV."

"I know where there's one," Emily offered. "It's in Delaware, about half an hour from here."

"Delaware Park?" Bob asked.

"Yes. I've been there once or twice. It has horse racing some days, and there's slot machines and gambling tables. They have a bunch of restaurants. What do you think?"

"I think I want to go. If it's alright with my son."

Catherine smiled at Bob. How could he refuse?

"Looks like we're going to Delaware Park," he said. "It'll be a first for both of us. Emily, you need to give me directions."

"No problem. We go south and follow Route 7 most of the way. I'll show you. Mrs. Bowie, be sure to take a sweater. Sometimes it's very chilly."

"Of course. I'll wear my gray blazer. That should work."

The trio exited Catherine's apartment, but not before she reached down to pat Mosely on the head. "I'll be back before the party," she told him. Emily and Bob raised their eyebrows and looked at each other. "Who knows?" the look seemed to say.

They signed themselves out at the reception desk, then Emily and Catherine waited while Bob drove his car round to pick them up.

The drive wasn't a long one. They traveled south on Kaolin Road, which eventually turned into Route 7, down through New Castle County into Pike Creek. They continued along Route 7 past modest brick homes and busy shopping centers. A few hundred yards from where Route 7 joined Route 4, they turned right onto Delaware Park Boulevard. This broad road wound through the White Clay Creek Country Club and its golf course, then to the parking lot for the casino. The lot was more than half full, so Bob dropped off Emily and his mom to avoid a long walk from the car.

Catherine was surprised to see that the building more resembled a warehouse than the fancy places she had walked past in Atlantic City. However, there was a large clean entrance with a white-pillared portico and valet parking available.

"Shall we go in?" Emily asked her.

"Yes, let's."

Emily held the heavy glass door for Catherine, who stopped immediately inside the entrance.

"What lights! What noise! Oh, I'm not sure I can handle this," she cried, grasping Emily's arm to steady herself. Her eyes tried to take in the pulsing white lights, the bursts of gold, and the flickers of bright red emanating from the long rows of slot machines.

"You'll get used to it after a few minutes," Emily reassured her, speaking above the din of bells ringing and buzzers going off at random.

At the entrance, they were only steps away from some of the most popular slot machines. Their cabinets soared up six and eight feet in the air and broadcast short videos of Michael Jackson, other pop music stars, or cartoon characters. Loud rock music was piped in and competed with the bells and whistles of the slot machines. Lights of all colors flashed in no particular order, and streams of people wandered by clutching plastic cups of tokens. Catherine was almost regretting her decision but not completely.

"We'll stand here for a minute and wait for Bob," Emily suggested, seeing Catherine's discomfort.

Catherine looked around. To her left, she saw escalators to an upper level and, past them, to a snack bar selling ice cream. She looked back to her right and saw a wall of smaller slot machines standing four or five feet tall and featuring smaller screens with ever-changing displays. *How do people choose which machine to play? she wondered.*

"Would you like to eat lunch first?" Emily asked. "I think that would be a good idea," Catherine replied. "I'm too bewildered by the noise and lights to decide what games to play."

"So you've never used a slot machine before?"

"No, never. I don't really approve of gambling, but so many people seem to enjoy it. I feel like I should at least try it once before I die."

"Well, you don't have to lose your money to a machine. It can go pretty fast that way. Delaware Park also has horse racing. It was a racetrack before it added the casino. If you want to have fun looking at the horses and the jockeys, you could always bet on the racehorses."

Bob arrived and said, "What now, ladies?"

"I think your mom would like to have lunch first," Emily said. "Follow me. I know just the place." Emily started walking into the throng of gamblers.

"Better take my arm, Mom," Bob said. "I don't want to lose you."

As they followed Emily past rows of slot machines into the depth of the first floor, Bob shouted to Emily, "I think you've been here more than once or twice."

"Well, maybe half a dozen times over the years."

Near the far end of the first floor, the piped-in music faded, along with the sounds of the slot machines. They passed a dance floor with a small stage. On the stage was a man who looked like Elvis. He wore a white jumpsuit studded with jewels and was swinging his hips as he belted out the words of *Jail House Rock.*

"Stop, stop," Catherine yelled. "I want to watch him."

A few people stood on the near side of a rope enclosure that defined the dance floor. Catherine, Bob, and Emily joined them at the satin blue rope strung between waist-high brass poles and watched the dancers out on the floor. A few couples were dancing the jitterbug. There were also a number of single women, mostly middle-aged, with bouffant hairdos, bosom-revealing sweaters, and skintight jeans tucked into black knee-high boots. They were having a ball, laughing with each other, and doing a dance Emily knew as the Pony around the wooden floor.

As Bob, Catherine, and Emily watched, Elvis, all the while singing, picked up some brightly colored scarves, stepped onto the dance floor, and danced among the ladies. The women loved it and got close to him but not close enough to hit him with their flapping elbows. Occasionally, Elvis picked someone to honor by taking a scarf from around his neck and placing it around the dancer's neck. Then he danced off to another group of women. After distributing all his scarves, Elvis returned to the stage and finished the song. Women clapped and hooted. Elvis bowed and disappeared into the stage wings.

"There'll be another show at four this afternoon," one of the musicians announced, and the band left the stage.

"That was fun," said Catherine. "Now, let's have some lunch."

Emily led them behind the stage's back wall to an escalator to the second level. They rode another one to the top level. She led them across the floor to the entrance of The Terrace, one of many restaurants in the building.

Looking in, they could see that the outside wall of the restaurant was made entirely of glass and looked down on the racetrack.

"Table for three," Emily told the hostess, who led them down a narrow aisle between the tables and down six steep steps. The steps descended to four levels. On each level was a long aisle with tables facing the window so that the guests at each table had an unobstructed view of the track. At the bottommost level, the hostess stood by a small table with an excellent view.

"Will this be okay?" she asked.

"Wonderful," said Emily, and turned to see Bob helping his mom, who was gingerly coming down the stairs. "Are you alright?" she asked. "I'd forgotten about the steps."

"I'm fine," Catherine said. "I love the view!"

After they sat down, the hostess passed around menus. "Your server will be here in a minute," she said.

"I can't believe I've never been here," Bob said. "No one at work ever mentioned this restaurant."

"It's a hidden gem," Emily said. "Lots of folks turn their noses up at racetracks, but the food is good here, and you get a show!"

Looking down at the brown dirt of the racing oval, they saw that horses were being led out onto the track. They came in pairs: one being the thoroughbred with a jockey onboard wearing colorful silks and an assigned number, the other a pony rider whose job was to guide the racehorse past the grandstand for the judges and betting patrons to view.

Emily fiddled with a small television-like box on their table. Soon they could see a close-up of the action on the track, accompanied by the announcer's running commentary of the horse's and jockey's names and a brief history of the horse's and the jockey's achievements.

"Can I bet on the horses?" Catherine asked. "Look at the large brown horse with the muscular hips. Number eight. I bet he's powerful. I want to bet on him."

Emily laughed and looked at Bob. His mother was really enjoying this.

Bob was looking a bit skeptical. *Is my dear, sweet mother really interested in betting on the ponies?* he was thinking.

"It's probably too late for this race now," Emily said. "But you can bet on the next race."

Their server arrived and handed them each a booklet. The booklets spelled out the participants in each race, the time the race would go off, who the jockey was, and the horses' and the jockeys' racing histories.

"Can I get you anything to drink?" the server asked.

"I'll have iced tea," Emily said.

"Same for me," said Bob.

"I'll have a whiskey sour," said Catherine. "On the rocks." To Bob's shocked face, she said, "I'm not driving, dear."

Emily loved it. She loved Mrs. Bowie; she loved Bob. This was turning out to be a perfectly wonderful afternoon.

They sat silently and enjoyed the horses and jockeys warming up around the track. Some of the horses were docile and sweet-tempered. Others were more rambunctious, trotting this way and that, and occasionally rearing up in the air. Emily pointed out that you could look at their numbers and match them up with the odds on the TV screen.

"That looks too complicated for me," Catherine said. "I want to enjoy looking at these beautiful animals."

"Did you ever ride?" Emily asked her.

"Maybe once or twice as a teenager, but that was just a tame walk through the woods with a camp counselor. How about you?"

"I had riding lessons when I was fourteen, and although I enjoyed it, the barn smells gave me an asthma attack. So I gave it up."

The server returned with their drinks as the horses made their slow-paced walk to the gate. Next, she took their food orders. Catherine ordered the turkey club, and Emily ordered the same. Bob got a burger. "Medium well," he instructed. Then they turned their attention back to the track.

The last horse had no sooner been coaxed into its spot when the gates opened and the announcer cried, "They're off!"

Emily had forgotten how much she enjoyed watching the horses take off at full gallop, pounding the dirt with their hooves and angling between each other for the best spot.

Horses who had led the pack at first faded into fourth and fifth place as other horses sped past them. It seemed only seconds for them to race around the entire oval and then surge forward at full gallop for the finish line. Just yards before the end, horse number eight, whose jockey wore pink and purple silks, came from behind with a burst of speed. He pounded past all the others and took the lead a millisecond before the finish line.

"He won! My horse won!" shouted Catherine.

"Good pick, Mom," Bob said. "Too bad we didn't have any money on that one. Let me know who you like for the next race, and I'll put our bets in."

"Be sure and look at your booklet," Emily said. "That was race number one, so look at the horses for race number two."

As they waited for their lunch, Emily examined the horses' names. She liked one called Silly Walks and another named Dancing Queen.

"I'm betting on The Judge," said Bob.

"Oh, I've got to see them first," Catherine said. She was looking at the TV screen where the next race participants were being led around a small wooded paddock with their numbers emblazoned on their saddle pads.

"I like the bay," she said. "Number five. What's his name?"

"Gray Ghost," said Emily. "He's beautiful. Now, you can bet on a horse at least three ways. For two dollars, you can bet on him to win, which is the largest payout, or you can bet on him to place, which means he comes in first or second, or you can bet on him to show, which means he comes in first, second, or third. That's the smallest payout."

"You know an awful lot about this," Bob said. "You hang out here often?"

Emily knew he was joking, but she answered him honestly. "I dated a guy who used to take me here instead of the movies or anywhere else, for that matter. I enjoyed it, but it was tiresome to come every Saturday. He said this was his life and what he liked to do. I'm afraid that relationship didn't last."

"I can see that." Bob grinned. "Now, have you ladies decided on your bets? I'll go buy the tickets."

"Gray Ghost for me," his mom said. "To win."

"Dancing Queen for me, to show," said Emily. "I'm a cautious bettor. I don't mind winning only a dollar or two."

Bob left. He returned quickly, handing tickets to Emily and Catherine. Just then, their food arrived. They ate silently, enjoying their lunch.

Five minutes later, the horses appeared on the track.

"Take your time eating," Emily said. "They walk around forever before they go to the gate."

She was right. The trio was done eating and wiping their mouths when the horses were finally in place.

"They're off!" said the announcer, and ten horses shot out of the gate, kicking up dust and bunching together as they headed down the track.

"Gray Ghost is in the lead!" Catherine said excitedly. "Keep it up," she called out as if the horse and his jockey in dark blue and aqua silks could hear her.

"Here come de Judge," joked Bob as his horse and jockey, in black and pink silks, pulled up on the outside of the pack.

"Dancing Queen looks like she's dancing and not running," groaned Emily as her horse pranced around in last place, almost as if she didn't know what she was there for.

"I think she reminds me of you," Bob joked. "Just having fun doing her own thing and the hell with what she's supposed to be doing."

"No way. You don't know what you're talking about," Emily kidded back. "And I think your horse is tired already." The Judge did seem to be slipping back into fifth or sixth place. Their horses were not even going to show, let alone win.

"He's got it! He's got it!" Catherine was shouting to Bob and Emily's amazement. She clutched Bob's arm in her excitement. She was practically bouncing up and down in her chair. "Go, Gray Ghost, go!" she urged the horse out loud and stood up for a better view of the finish line. All the restaurant patrons turned to look at this elderly woman caught up in the drama of the race.

"He won! My horse won!" Catherine crowed as Gray Ghost passed the finish line a nose hair ahead of the dark horse in second place. She stood up, grabbed Bob's shoulder and bounced on her toes. "I can't believe it. I won the very first time!"

"Let's sit down and see how much," Bob said solemnly, but he was secretly glad his mother was having such a good time. He couldn't remember when he'd ever seen his mother have so much fun.

"Oh yes, oh yes! How much did I win?"

"They'll announce it in a minute and show it on the screen here," Emily said.

The server arrived with their bill.

"Dessert?" she asked.

"I don't think so," said Catherine. "I'm too excited to eat."

"The check is all," said Bob, giving the server his credit card.

"I put ten dollars down on each horse," Bob said. "But I forget what the odds were for each of them."

As they left the restaurant, Bob stopped at the payout window and returned with twenty-five dollars for his mother.

"The odds were five to two, and I bet ten dollars, so you won twenty-five dollars. I don't know how that works out exactly, but they must know what they're doing." He turned to Emily, "Do you know how the odds work, Miss Delaware Park?"

"Well, I'm not sure. I think it's five dollars for every two-dollar bet, so that works out about right."

"I forgot you were a math whiz," he joked as his mom put the money in her purse.

"Oh, thank you so much, both of you," she said. "But I'm tired now. Can we go back? I want to have a short lie down before the party this afternoon. Will you both stay for it?"

Emily looked at Bob, raised her eyebrows, and smiled as if to say, "Yes, I'd be glad to stay."

"Of course, Mom. We'd love to. Now watch your step on these escalators."

When they reached the ground floor, they headed back the way they came in. The dance floor was empty and the stage dark. Catherine was not so bothered by the lights and noise now. As they neared the entrance, she stopped in front of a machine with a screen displaying rows of squares with a picture of a different puppy in half the squares, the other squares being filled with hearts, diamonds, cherries, or the number seven.

"I have to play just once," she turned and said to Bob. "Can I?"

"I'm not sure how we do this," Bob said. "I don't have any tokens."

"I'll take care of it," Emily said and took a five-dollar bill from her purse. She fed it into the machine and then pressed a button that read "1X." She smiled. "Now pull the handle of the machine."

Catherine reached up and yanked down the silver handle. She stood transfixed as the rows of squares spun around and then stopped. Each square had a different picture.

"What happens next?" she asked Emily.

"You didn't win anything," Emily explained. "Try it again."

Catherine repeated her pull and watched the squares spin. They came to a stop, and suddenly, they heard bells ringing. A red light at the top of the machine began to pulse and spin around.

"What's happened?" Catherine asked. "Did I break the machine?"

"You won!" Emily laughed and pointed at the screen where five of the same puppy in a row were lined up and edged with white lights.

"How much?" Bob asked.

"Two hundred and thirty dollars!" Emily whooped. "Look down there at the bottom of the screen. Do you believe it? Your second try, and you won two hundred and thirty dollars!"

"But where is it?" Catherine sounded worried. "I don't see any coins coming out of the machine."

"The machine prints out a voucher that you take to the Redemption window," Emily explained. "Are you ready to go, or do you want to play some more?"

"Oh, I'm ready to go. I believe in quitting while you're ahead."

"Smart woman," Emily said. "Here's what you do," and she showed her where to push the "cash out" button. A small piece of paper emerged from the top of the machine. Catherine grabbed it and read "$233."

"Where did the extra three dollars come from?" she asked Emily.

"We put five dollars in, and the bets were each one dollar. You didn't win anything with your first dollar, but you won two hundred and thirty dollars with the next dollar bet. So you get the two hundred and thirty plus the three dollars you didn't use to bet."

"Your math skills are amazing," Catherine told her and squeezed her arm. "You must come and balance my checkbook sometime."

"I'd be glad to," Emily said. "Now let's head to the Redemption area and get your money.

The Redemption area was crowded and they had to stand in line. While waiting, Emily glanced at the other casino patrons patiently awaiting their turn.

Suddenly her attention was caught by two security guards escorting a man out of the building. The gentleman was sandwiched between the guards. While they weren't manhandling him, the security guards' shoulders pressed firmly against those of the unwanted visitor. As the gentleman began to protest that he was being treated unfairly, Emily recognized him and gasped; it was Edward Weir, L'Automne's director.

Emily nudged Bob and tapped Catherine's shoulder to show them what was happening. When the security guards got to the glass doors of the exit, they stood back and let the man leave unmolested. Weir's dignity was obviously damaged; he took a moment to collect himself and square his shoulders. Without a backward glance, he patted his hair and marched into the parking lot.

"That was the director!" Bob said to his mom.

"Oh my," she responded. "What has he gotten himself into?"

"Have there been any rumors of him gambling?" Bob asked.

"No, but then most of the staff would probably go to casinos in Pennsylvania rather than Delaware," she said. "Maybe he thought no one would recognize him here."

It was Catherine's turn at the Redemption window, and she gingerly pushed her ticket through the slot under the glass divider.

"How would you like this, ma'am?" asked the clerk.

"Twenties will be fine," she said and opened her purse to make room for the money.

Emily kept her eyes on the surrounding crowds to make sure no one noticed how much money Catherine put in her purse. She was glad Bob was there to discourage any ne'er-do-wells who might follow them into the parking lot and try to take advantage of an elderly woman.

After snapping her purse shut, Catherine walked between Bob and Emily to the exit.

"I think we should all walk to the car together," Emily suggested.

"I don't want your mom and me left alone with all this money in her purse."

"Good idea," Bob said. "The car's not far."

"Why do you suppose those men were escorting Mr. Weir out the door?" Catherine asked.

"They might have caught him trying to cheat," Bob said.

"I wonder if he could have stolen Rawley's two hundred dollars," Catherine said. *And my credit card*, she thought.

"Sounds like a possibility," Emily replied, thinking of all the other things he might be responsible for, maybe even Shay's murder. Not wanting to upset Mrs. Bowie, she kept these thoughts to herself.

CHAPTER TWENTY-THREE

Catherine didn't notice Bob and Emily exchanging concerned looks as they reached Bob's SUV and climbed in. They said little as they rode up Route 7 and into Pennsylvania. At one point, Catherine said, "I'm pretty tired after all that excitement. What time is it? Do I have time for a nap before the Halloween party?"

"It's two-thirty now," Bob replied. "We'll be back by three. So I guess you could nap for an hour until four and have half an hour to get ready."

"That should be plenty of time. Are you two staying for the party?"

"We don't have costumes," Emily said.

"Well, you've got a few hours to find some. I'd really love for you to be there."

"We'll figure something out, won't we, Bob?"

"Looks like a trip to Walmart is in order," he replied.

After dropping off Catherine, Bob said, "I hope you don't mind going to this party. I'm really worried about my mom. I want to be there with her as much as possible."

"I agree," Emily said. "I'm glad we will be."

Bob headed to Walmart. They went north into Kennett Square and east on Cypress, eventually joining Route 1. Walmart came up quickly on the left.

Sitting in the parking lot, Bob said, "This is where they found Shay, in the dumpster behind the store."

"I know. It's kind of creepy our coming here, but I don't know where else we'd go."

"Well, let's get this over with," Bob said, opening the door. "I hope there's something decent left for us. I don't want to go as Superman or a Teletubby."

"Tinky Winky was the biggest one. I think you'd make a perfect Tinky Winky."

"How do you know this stuff? Do you watch children's programs on Saturday mornings?"

"No, but sometimes I come upon them when I'm flipping through the stations. And when all the uproar started about their being dangerous for young children to watch, I had to check them out."

"And are they dangerous?"

"No way. They're just cute. And nonthreatening."

"Not like me?" Bob joked as he held the Walmart door open for her.

"Never."

They didn't need to look far for costumes. A huge display with a "50% off" sale sign was staged ten feet inside the entrance. The costumes were picked over and disordered, mixing children's costumes with the adults'.

They spent many minutes pulling out costumes that looked big enough for them and found several possibilities.

"Shall I be a sexy nurse, a sexy kitten, or a Disney Princess?" Emily asked Bob, holding up three costumes, although the first two had very little fabric dangling from their plastic hangers. The Disney Princess was a full-length dress with a scooped blue bodice, puffy sleeves, and a yellow satiny skirt.

"Considering the crowd, I'd have to vote for the Disney Princess."

"And have you found a Teletubby costume yet?"

"No, only Superman, Spiderman, and a Policeman."

"I vote Policeman, Tinky Winky's alter ego."

"I agree. And I don't think I'd look good in tights."

They took their purchases to the checkout counter. Emily insisted she pay for them. "After all, you paid for lunch," she pointed out.

"We still have half an hour before Mom wants to get up from her nap. How about we stop for a drink?"

"That would be heavenly. Let's go back to the Kennett Square Inn. We can sit at the bar." Emily hoped she would see Letty again, especially since it was Halloween.

"Great idea," Bob agreed and, within minutes, they were parking on State Street.

The Inn was deserted this late in the afternoon, but a young woman was behind the bar and eager to serve them.

"A glass of Pinot Grigio and a glass of water," Emily ordered.

"I'll take a Molson's," said Bob.

While waiting for their drinks, Emily glanced at the bar stool where she'd seen Letty but was dismayed to find she wasn't there. *Perhaps she's in Philadelphia today,* she thought.

Drinks arrived, and they sat quietly for a while, enjoying the colonial atmosphere of the inn. There was no music and the lights were low, creating a golden glow from the Windsor chairs and pine paneling. Emily sighed with happiness. What a great day this had been. She had spent the time with the man she loved and his surprisingly fun-loving mother. She had enjoyed every moment at Delaware Park, even though she hadn't won any money. Bob's mom was delightful, and Emily was glad for her beginner's luck.

"A penny for your thoughts," Bob said, bringing her out of her reverie.

"It's been such a wonderful day! I love your mom. I hope she wins every time we take her to Delaware Park."

"I'm glad you've enjoyed yourself. Now finish up; it's almost four." He smiled.

As Bob settled the bill, the overhead lights suddenly went out. Luckily the candles at each of the tables cast enough light that Bob and Emily could see each other.

"What now?" a masculine voice said. "Another blown fuse?"

"Look out the window," said a woman. "All the streetlights and storefronts are dark."

"Must be all of Kennett," the man replied.

Bob and Emily could see their way to the door. Once outside they were buffeted by a chilly gust of wind. Looking up, they saw dark storm clouds rolling in from the west and blocking the sky. The air felt ten degrees cooler than it had before they entered the Inn. Suddenly a lightning bolt flashed across the sky followed by an immediate boom. The storm was upon them.

Luckily, Bob's SUV was parked out front. The rain began a moment after they shut the doors. Both sighed with relief.

"That was close," Bob said. "We almost got soaked."

"Let's hope it lets up a bit when we get to L'Automne," Emily replied.

It was an eerie drive from the restaurant on State Street to the intersection with South Union. A few cars crept beside them, their headlights reflected in the dark storefronts and in the thick drops of rain. Bob and Emily felt like they were in a bizarre sci-fi movie set in a desolate future.

The traffic light was out, and Bob had to wait to turn left onto South Union. Fortunately, all the drivers going west and south were being cautious. He drove slowly under the canopy of old trees that arched over South Union, their branches heavy with rain and swaying in the wind. The towering row homes on either side were also dark, except for candlelight sporadically filtering through curtains.

By proceeding slowly, Bob was able to find the access road to L'Automne. They drove carefully up the darkened drive with only the headlights to help Bob find the road's edges. As they neared the facility, Emily viewed the looming mansion with trepidation. All the windows were dark. The only light shone from the lobby windows. The crenellated roof stood out against the black sky like a castle of doom, a place where Count Dracula would just be awakening.

"Shouldn't they have a generator?" Emily asked.

"You would think so. Maybe they haven't found the 'On' switch yet."

Emily wasn't sure if she were meant to laugh at this, so she said nothing.

Hurriedly they grabbed their shopping bags and jumped from the car, running as best they could in the wind and the rain, the distance from the car to the entrance.

Bob and Emily walked into a scene of muted chaos. No one was at the reception desk, but an industrial-sized flashlight had been left on the counter so people could see. As they walked further into the lobby, they heard a "whomp." Spotlights placed in central areas of the building suddenly came on, and the lobby lit up.

Carved pumpkins had been placed on the reception desk and on furniture in the lounge. Long strips of orange and black crepe paper streamed down from the ceiling over the lounge, cutting the light into ribbons. The leering jack-o'-lanterns and filtered light gave Emily the shivers. She asked, "Where are all the people?"

As Emily and Bob walked farther, they found people gathered in the dining room. Four spotlights, one in each corner, angled out to illuminate the center of the room, leaving the four corners dark. Tables were arranged against a wall with serving trays of food for a buffet dinner. A loud murmur rose from the costumed residents as they crowded together and looked to each other for answers.

The servers weren't in costume, but they were dressed in black shirts and pants and wore black eye masks. They could have easily disappeared into the shadows and didn't seem disturbed by the commotion. They were busily arranging plates and napkins.

"Let's go see my mom," Bob said. "We'll have to take the stairs."

Luckily, there were spotlights on the staircase and in the hall. They knocked at Catherine's apartment and heard her respond, "Come in!" Opening the door, they gasped. Illuminated by the light of half a dozen candles, Catherine appeared in front of them dressed as Glinda, the Good Witch, in a billowing pink dress covered with silver stars. She wore a wig of long golden hair under a tall silver crown. In her hand, she held a silver wand topped with a silver star. She shone like an angel just descended into the dim evening light.

"You look lovely!" Emily exclaimed, clapping her hands.

"Stunning," said Bob.

Catherine responded by touching them each on the head with her silver wand. "Bless you, my children."

"So I guess they're going ahead with the party despite the power outage," Bob said.

"Oh yes," said Catherine. "Now I see you have costumes. Go get changed."

CHAPTER TWENTY-FOUR

While Emily and Bob were changing, they heard the telephone ring.

Catherine answered it. After saying "Hello" and "Yes, that's me," she was quiet, listening intently.

When Bob and Emily finished dressing, they came out of the bedroom to hear Catherine say, "Thank you, I appreciate your letting me know."

She set down the receiver and turned to Bob and Emily.

"Let me guess! Princess and Policeman. You both look wonderful."

"Thank you," said Bob and Emily together.

"That was a nice young man from my credit card company," Catherine explained, nodding at the phone. "They have the name and address of the homeowner where my credit card was used to pay for utilities. It was our director, Mr. Weir. Do you believe it!"

"That wasn't too smart on his part," Emily said. "Didn't he figure out that they would use the address from the utility to track him down?"

"He must have been desperate, what with his gambling and all," Catherine said, shaking her head. "He must have needed to pay for those utilities for his family."

"I'm glad at least one question has been answered," sighed Bob.

"But he needs to be punished!" Catherine said.

"You may have to file a complaint with the police," Emily offered.

"Have you had this happen to you, dear?" Catherine asked.

"Not credit card theft. My gold jewelry was stolen by employees of a cleaning company. I complained to the company, they called the police, and the police discovered who the culprits were. I had to go to the police station and file a complaint."

"Did you get your jewelry back?" Bob asked.

"No. The person who stole it went immediately to a pawn shop and got cash for the jewelry. Pawn shops are supposed to wait eighteen days before selling items brought in, but a few skirt the law. Unfortunately, my thief went to one of those. I spoke to an officer who said they believed the jewelry had immediately been sold and melted down for the gold."

"Was the thief prosecuted?" Catherine asked.

"I got a letter a few months later telling me someone was formally charged, but I haven't heard anything since then."

"Well, I'd like to have the satisfaction of seeing the director punished for stealing my credit card," Catherine said. "Although I have to feel sorry for anyone so in need of paying their utilities that they would steal from an old lady. Luckily, I have enough in the checking account to pay the credit card, but the young man said they will remove the charges, and I should deduct the amount from the balance. Do you think I should go to Weir's office and confront him?"

"Not this afternoon," Bob said. "Let it wait until tomorrow morning. You don't want any drama to spoil the party for everyone this afternoon."

"Well, that sounds best. I don't exactly look threatening, do I?" Catherine spun around on her toes.

"Neither do we." Emily smiled, considering her princess costume. "Although Bob might be accused of impersonating an officer."

"If you need money, Mom," Bob said, "you know you can ask me."

"Thank you, Son, but I'm fine. Now let's get to this party. We're already late."

Bob and Emily helped Catherine extinguish the candles. Making for the door, she stopped to pet Mosely. Then she gathered her billowing pink skirt, careful not to disturb its silver stars, and walked carefully into the hallway. Bob and Emily followed her and nodded at residents leaving their rooms dressed as pirates, witches, airline pilots, and nurses. They were a colorful group, filling the hallway and staircase with their fake daggers, wands, and oversize hats.

"No one," Emily whispered to Catherine, "Looks as beautiful as you."

When they arrived at the bottom of the stairs, it was apparent that Shay's expertise as an Activities Coordinator was sorely missed. People wandered around in the lobby unsure where to go or what to do next. In the dining room, food was laid out on the buffet tables, but anyone who ventured near the chicken breasts and pork ribs heard Lord Johnston, dressed as Ebenezer Scrooge, bark "Dinner isn't ready yet! Go down to the Activities Room!"

Nichole Drago, dressed as a biker chick in a leather vest decorated with silver chains and her trademark black leather pants, took charge and started ushering people out of the dining room and down the broad marble stairs.

"I'm sure the power will be back soon," she was reassuring them.

"Where's the director?" Bob asked her.

"I've no idea. But the maintenance man is working on getting our electricity back."

"All of Kennett is in the dark," Emily told her.

"Oh dear," Nichole replied. "Then it may be a while before it's restored."

Catherine, Bob, and Emily waited to go down last. As they started down the stairs, they saw a man enter the building and speak to the nurse's aide manning the reception desk.

"That's Detective Hudson!" Catherine told them. "He spoke to us when Shay was killed."

"Let's wait here a minute," Emily said.

Bob felt a bit awkward. He was worried Detective Hudson might mistake him for a fellow policeman or be offended at his costume. Neither happened. They watched the nurse's aide direct Detective Hudson to the stairs to the lower level.

"Let's talk to him," Emily said and took off before Bob could protest. "Detective Hudson," Emily called out.

Hudson turned to look at her. His eyes widened slightly, noticing her costume, but he said nothing.

"Hi, I'm Emily Menotti. My boyfriend is the son of a resident here. Do you know why the power is out all over Kennett?"

"Lightning hit a power substation. They're predicting a one-to-two-hour repair time. I wanted to check on everybody here."

"Thank you! We appreciate that," Catherine said, catching up to Emily.

Emily continued, "Have there been any breaks in the case? Have you caught whoever killed Shay Dinsmore?"

"I'm not supposed to comment on an investigation," he said.

Emily noticed Bob had disappeared. *Embarrassed by his costume,* she thought.

"Well, can you tell us if anyone is in danger here?"

"No, I really can't," he said. Then added, "Sorry, I have to go. I need to check out the building."

"Thanks, anyway," Emily said, disappointed. She turned to look for Bob.

Bob suddenly appeared. He had been hiding in the dining room. "Let's go dazzle your friends, Mom," Bob said, and they made for the stairs.

On the lower level, they could see that the Activities Room was lit with corner spotlights angled out to the center as the other rooms had been. Nichole Drago greeted them and handed them each a slip of paper and a pencil. The paper listed various categories of costume competition: Prettiest, Scariest, and Most Imaginative. There was a space next to each to write in your candidate.

"We're carrying on with our Halloween party and costume competition as planned," she told them. "Put these ballots in that big black box on the table behind me when you're done. We'll award prizes at five o'clock and then go upstairs to eat. You can get a glass of wine or soda at the bar in the far corner."

"Thank you, Nichole," Catherine said. "You're filling in nicely for Shay. I'm sure we all appreciate it."

"Someone had to do it," she said, smiling at the compliment. "Now go have fun.

Catherine said, "Let's circulate first. I want to see everyone's costumes before I vote."

The trio began to make a circuit of the room. Emily felt a shiver of apprehension as they wandered among the crowd, passing in and out of the shadows created by the corner spotlights. For all anyone knew, the killer could be hiding among them. To quell her fears she commented on the people they passed.

"She's a beautiful queen. I'm going to guess Victoria," said Emily, pointing out a large handsome woman in a black brocade gown, blue satin sash, and white veil topped with an ornate small gold crown encircled with pearls.

"That's Mrs. Gildenstern," said Catherine. "Quite appropriate if you knew her. She likes to lord it over everyone."

"And there's Jack the Ripper, I think," said Bob, nodding toward a tall thin gentleman in a top hat and black overcoat. Dark greasy strands of hair stuck out below his hat and over the dark scarf wrapped around the lower half of his face. He carried a twelve-inch plastic knife covered in fake blood. He'd put black makeup under his eyes that, added to the scarf and top hat, created a powerful disguise.

Heavens, thought Emily. *I hope that's not our killer flaunting his prowess.*

"Who's that, Mom?" Bob asked, nodding at the gentleman in question.

"I have no idea; his disguise is so good. I think I'll vote for him as the scariest."

The rest of the crowd was an assortment of elderly nurses, doctors, witches, and aging superheroes, perhaps alter egos of the costume wearers. Emily noticed that Catherine knew most of the crowd by name and stopped to exchange pleasantries, but there was no one she spoke to in a good-friend way. She guessed Rawley Bingham, Sr. must be her only best friend.

As they completed their circuit around the floor, they stopped at the black box and deposited their ballots.

"You're just in time," Nichole Drago said. "I'm about to count the votes."

"Let's get something to drink," Catherine suggested.

"Amen to that," replied Bob.

They went to the bar and ordered three white wines, which were served in tiny plastic cups.

"They certainly didn't go all out with the refreshments," Catherine whispered to Emily.

"How is your friend, Rawley, doing?" Emily asked. "Is he out of the hospital?"

"I think he came home this afternoon. His son called and asked me not to come by. Rawley Jr. is staying with him tonight. He said his father is still quite shook up and needs to rest."

"That's understandable, but it's too bad he's missing the party," Bob said.

"Well, he's not much of a party person anyway," Catherine replied.

They heard a series of loud raps and saw Nichole Drago calling for everyone's attention.

"I'm going to announce the winners," she said.

"Winner for Scariest Costume is Jeremy Brown with, what we assume, is his interpretation of Jack the Ripper."

Everyone clapped as Jeremy Brown came forward to accept his prize: a bottle of wine.

"Thank you all," he said and then brandished his knife. "Be sure and lock your doors tonight. I may be on the prowl."

Emily shivered. She whispered to Catherine, "Let's hope he didn't kill Shay Dinsmore."

Catherine laughed and said, "Now that I know who it is, I wouldn't worry. He wouldn't hurt a fly."

"Next category, Prettiest," said Nichole. "And the winner is Catherine Bowie for her Glinda the Good Witch costume. And we all know what a good witch she is!" The crowd broke out in applause.

Catherine glided her way to Nichole, the crowd making room for her huge pink skirt. It made a soft, rustling noise as she brushed past. "Thank you so much," Catherine said and lifted her bottle of wine above her head. "Wait until you see what I wear next year!"

Everyone clapped, and Nichole spoke again, "For Most Imaginative, the winner is The Walking Dead. And I have to admit, folks, I don't know who this is."

The crowd parted to let a woman through whose ghostly appearance gliding in from the shadows truly did create chills. She wore a wig of flowing white hair, dirty and matted, that hung down and covered her chest. Circling the crown of her head was a garland of dead white roses. Her dress was a floor-length shroud of grayish-white linen. Two thin arms emerged, wearing dirty long white gloves. Frayed strands of rope hung from her shoulders and crisscrossed her body. But the scariest part of her was her face, painted white, with bloodless lips. Her eyes were hidden behind a narrow cloth mask tied around her head. Thin slits for vision were cut in the center of two large luminous orange eyes with glowing white irises. Emily was duly impressed by the ingenuity it would have taken to create those eyes and this illusion of life amidst death.

As the creature accepted her bottle of wine, Nichole Drago asked, "Tell us who you are."

"I'm someone who's come back from the dead," the soft voice replied. "Can't you guess?"

Everyone in the crowd began to murmur and look at each other. "Can it be Shay?" was heard to echo through the room. Noise and movement in the back of the room grabbed the crowd's attention, and everyone turned to see what was happening there.

CHAPTER TWENTY-FIVE

Back to Sunday Night Walmart's Parking Lot

Shay heard the tap on her car window and rolled it down. The motorcyclist was standing there, the cold mist floating all around him and highlighting his pale hair. He looked like an angel surrounded by the eerie glow of the mercury vapor lamps. Shay could see herself reflected in the lenses of his wrap-around sunglasses.

"Can I talk to you?" the angel asked in a halting voice.

"Sure. Come around and get in the passenger side." Shay hit the unlock button to let him in.

The motorcyclist slowly walked around the front of the car to the passenger side. Once inside, he slammed the door shut and looked around the parking lot to check if he'd been seen. No cars were nearby, and no one lounged along the store walls. He was nervous. He was determined not to make the mistakes he'd seen in so many detective movies. Before Shay said a word, the angel gave her a smile that, just for a nanosecond, frightened Shay. Then he removed his sunglasses.

Shay gasped. It wasn't a he at all. He was a she who took advantage of Shay's shock to quickly thrust a needle into the side of Shay's neck and push down the plunger. Shay was stunned and didn't react, and the killer threw the needle on the floor.

She expected Shay to pass out immediately, but Shay didn't.

Instead, Shay began struggling to undo her seat belt and get out of the car. The killer couldn't let her get away, so she put her hands around Shay's throat and began to choke her.

Shay was usually quick and wiry, but on this cold night, she had worn a thick wool coat over a bulky knit sweater. She was tightly jammed between the car seat and the steering wheel and locked into place by her seat belt. She raised her arms with difficulty and was able to force her own hands over those of her adversary to try and pull them away. But the woman was too quick. She wore only a slim leather jacket, which didn't hinder her arms. She had hoisted herself onto her knees as she leaned in and applied pressure to Shay's throat. Shay clawed at the hands, feeling the thin leather gloves. Her own hands were shoved into mittens that rendered them mostly ineffective. Worst of all, Shay was beginning to feel woozy.

The woman was small and extremely motivated and maintained the pressure on Shay's throat, even shoving one knee against Shay to further incapacitate her. This angel of death knew strangling someone took more time than it did in films. She had been strengthening her hands and shoulders for months. She could exert continual pressure on Shay's windpipe, despite Shay's feeble thrashing in the confined space of the driver's seat.

Shay wanted to speak. She wanted to scream. She wanted to get a knee or a punch in, but she couldn't do any of those things. She tried to twist and squirm away from her attacker, but there was nowhere to go. She was feeling sleepy now, almost ready to nod off. The powerful hands tightened around Shay's throat; the attacker's knee pressed into Shay's side. So Shay did the only thing she could. She looked at the angel with pleading eyes begging her to stop. However, there was no stopping, and after forty-five interminable seconds, Shay blacked out.

The woman continued applying pressure until Shay had been limp for some time. Because of the dark, she couldn't look for purple blotches on the skin or red dots in the eyes. She thought Shay's tongue might be swollen by now, but she couldn't be sure in the dim light. She kept her hands around her neck even after Shay ceased struggling, counting slowly to three hundred. Her research had told her that a person could take up to five minutes to die of strangulation. She had to be sure.

When she reached three hundred, she loosened her grip and watched Shay slump forward. The killer looked around again and saw no one. She got out, reached in, and undid Shay's seatbelt. After pulling Shay's body over to the passenger seat, she closed the door. Going around to the driver's side, she got in and started the engine. Still looking carefully for anyone who might see her, she drove Shay's car to the back of the Walmart building where the dumpsters were kept. She pulled up to one, got out, and threw up the dumpster lid. Then she opened the car door, brought out Shay's body, and shoved her against the dumpster. It wasn't easy, but the woman managed to push the body up and over the lip of the bin, waiting to hear the body fall inside.

The woman closed the passenger door and went to the driver's side. She drove the car to the far side of the parking lot, closer to Route 1, where trees created shadows on the ground. She parked the car in the darkest spot she could find, left the keys in, got out, and slammed the door shut. She took one last quick look around and didn't see anyone. She returned to her motorcycle and rode away.

The witch and the scarecrow in the back seat of Shay's car sat still and silent with their sewn-on smiles and grinning eyes that had seen so much and could say so little.

CHAPTER TWENTY-SIX
Return to The Halloween Party

"Hi, Ed, remember me?"

She had come up behind him as he stood in the shadows at the back of the room while the crowd watched the costume awards. She whispered in his ear again, "Darling."

He knew that voice, but it couldn't be. He turned to see a woman disguised as a black witch, but a beautiful one. She had long silken dark hair and a mask made of black lace. He could see only her large blue eyes and the small cutouts of her fair skin. Her dress was a slender drape of silky black fabric with dark ribbons crisscrossed on the bodice. The sleeves were wrist length and billowed out from her elbows. Her hands lay hidden in soft black gloves. Confused, Weir couldn't picture who the black-haired, blue-eyed beauty could be. But he thought he recognized the voice. He started to feel moist and uncomfortable.

"No, I don't know who you are," he said.

"It's me, Tina Tuesday. Tess's sister." She whispered this softly, close to his ear. She didn't want anyone to overhear them.

"I thought you were dead," he replied and mumbled, "And a blonde." He felt panic flaring up inside his stomach and up through his chest. He and Tina had had a session or two alone in his office before she disappeared to Mexico with her boyfriend. He had bragged repeatedly to his friends about screwing both twins.

"It's a wig, darling. Oh, how I've missed lusting after your little cat mouth." The witch began to kiss him.

Weir placed his hands on the satin-clad hips and leaned into the kiss. Whoever this was, she was desirable.

The witch drew her head back. "Not so fast, lover boy," she crooned. "Tess wrote to me about you and Shay. You wasted no time replacing Tess in your affections once she got sick. I think we're owed some penance."

"What do you mean?" A tiny spasm of fear erupted in Weir's gut. He tried to ignore it.

The witch drew him to her now and pressed her hips into his, waiting for the proper response. It happened quickly and she knew the time was right. As Weir moaned into her neck, she brought up her knee, pulled it back, and thrust hard into his groin. Weir yelped in pain and staggered back. Clutching himself, he fell to the floor. Hearing Weir's cry of pain, the woman in the walking-dead costume pushed through the crowd and rushed over to kneel beside him. She cradled his head in her arms.

"What happened?" she asked. "Are you okay?"

The black witch knelt on his opposite side. She also seemed solicitous until, using her billowing sleeves as cover, she drew out a needle and jabbed it in his neck. It was a much more powerful dose than the ones she'd used before. She had learned a thing or two.

"Ow!" Weir cried out and then went limp.

Standing only a few feet away, Emily had turned when she heard Weir scream the first time. She saw the woman in white arrive and kneel beside him. Then she thought she saw the woman in black kneel, pull something from her sleeve, and apply it to Weir's neck.

Hearing the screams and seeing the figures in the corner, the crowd turned and gasped at the scene.

"No need to worry," the black witch announced to them. "He fainted. I'll take care of him." She bent over him and began to caress his head. "Wake up, darling," she crooned, her body hiding the dead Weir.

"You've killed him!" the woman in white shouted and took off her mask with the painted orange eyes.

"You!" said the black witch and pulled off her black lace mask.

The twins stared at each other, and a look passed between them. It was not a look of sisterly affection. Neither said another word. These twins didn't need words to communicate their emotions. They sat there still as stone, with the lifeless Weir lying between them.

Emily stood over the black witch. "You did something to him, didn't you?" Then she knelt and noticed the needle mark on Weir's neck. She touched Weir's carotid artery. There was no pulse. He was already a mottled blue. She didn't think CPR would help him now.

"Someone call 911," Emily shouted. To those standing by, she said, "I think he's dead."

"No, he's not; he passed out," the witch said. "I'll get some smelling salts from the nurse." She stood up. "I'll be right back."

"No, you won't." Emily stood up and put her hands around the witch's arm, holding her tightly.

"Let me go! I'm trying to save his life!"

"Anyone can see he's dead. You've killed him!" Emily tightened her grip.

"Let me go." The witch twisted and tried to struggle free.

"Officer, arrest this woman," shouted Emily, hoping Detective Hudson was somewhere nearby. Her hands slid on the silky black fabric, making it difficult for Emily to keep hold of the woman. She looked for Bob. "She's a killer."

"And he was a thief!" the witch cried out. "A filthy cheater and an embezzler. He was stealing from you all." She tried again to wrench free of Emily. "He deserved to die!"

"And Shay?" Emily asked. She held each arm now. They made a bizarre tableau, like a scene from an animated fairy tale, the princess fighting the wicked witch.

"She was his accomplice!"

"Officer!" Emily shouted again, and Bob roused himself from his paralyzing shock at what was taking place. He decided that whatever was happening, he needed to act even if he wasn't a real policeman. "Find Detective Hudson. He's in the building," he said to those around him, stepping forward to help Emily hold the witch. He looked down at Weir and saw that he was lifeless.

"Is the nurse here?" he called out. "A *real* nurse," he added on second thought. "Someone needs to check on this man. I'll stay here and hold on to this woman, whoever she is."

"I'm Tess," said the witch.

"No, I'm Tess," said the woman in white. "The real Tess. She's Tina."

Nichole Drago appeared now. She had had enough of someone else controlling the show. "Who are you? Tell the truth!" she demanded of the two women.

Neither spoke.

A pirate sauntered over and looked at the women closely. "Now I know what struck me as funny about you," he told the black witch.

"Who do you think you are?" she demanded.

"You know me. I'm Stanley Cubbage, the maintenance man." The pirate pulled off the bandanna covering his face's lower half.

"You are not Tess. Tess has a mole on her right cheek, and your mole is on the left."

"And who is this—the woman who looks like the walking dead?" asked Nichole.

"The real Tess Tuesday," the pirate replied. "She's got the mole on her right cheek. Tina here has been masquerading as Tess. When she didn't remember my fixing her wheelchair, I knew something was up. Then I remembered her mole and saw it on the wrong cheek."

"But the real Tess needs a wheelchair," Emily spoke up. "We understood that she has MS."

"I'm in remission. The clinic in Mexico healed me," replied the woman in white. "Now I want my job back. Sorry, Tina," she said. "The masquerade is up."

The crowd parted as Detective Hudson came through. He gave Bob an odd look. Bob was still clutching the witch's arm.

"It's a costume," Bob explained.

"I'll take over from here," Hudson said. He knelt and examined Weir, whose body was fading from blue to gray.

"Someone called an ambulance," Emily spoke up.

"Too late for that, I'm afraid," said Detective Hudson. "I'll tell the EMTs to call the coroner. Now, everyone, please step back and give me some room. I'll need to speak to you all eventually."

"You need to arrest this one," Emily said, indicating Tina dressed as a witch.

"She's responsible for Weir?" he asked.

"And probably Shay also," Emily said.

Tina didn't protest as Hudson put handcuffs on her.

Catherine came up to Emily and hugged her.

"Thank goodness you and Bob were here," she said.

As if to emphasize Catherine's relief, all the lights suddenly came on and blinded everyone with their brightness. People blinked their eyes as if waking up to bright sun, and a few were tempted to think that Weir's murder had all been a bad dream.

Then everyone was startled by shouting and all turned to see what was happening. It was Ebenezer Scrooge yelling, "Time to eat, folks. Please go to the dining room. Bah humbug!"

CHAPTER TWENTY-SEVEN
Thursday Evening, November 1

Five people sat in the living room of Rawley Bingham, Sr.: Rawley Sr., his son, Catherine Bowie, Bob, and Emily. Each held a glass with a generous pour of white wine, except for Rawley Sr., who was still taking powerful meds.

"Do you mind going over all this again for my benefit?" Rawley Jr. asked. "We've only gotten bits and pieces of the story from everyone else. We know about the attack on Weir, but we don't understand why."

"I'll let Emily do the honors," Bob said and gave her a nod.

"Thanks, Bob. I think I've got it straight now after talking to Detectives Cortez and Hudson earlier today. Shay was killed by Tina Tuesday, who everybody thought was Tess. Tina, as Tess, told everyone that her twin had eloped to Mexico to be with her boyfriend. The real Tess had gone to Mexico, but not with a boyfriend. She went to a clinic near Mexico City that has successfully treated MS.

"Tina wasn't working at the time and decided to take her twin's place without telling anyone who she was. She even taught herself how to get around in a wheelchair. Tess said she didn't mind. She didn't know how long she'd be staying in Mexico, and this way, her job would be waiting for her when she got back."

"As a lawyer, I've seen twins surreptitiously change places before," commented Rawley Jr.

"Tina was able to get away with this deception," Emily continued, "because Tess had told her about everything and everyone here at L'Automne. Tina thought she could pull it off. She also decided, unfortunately, to collect Tess's disability checks instead of forwarding them to Tess. Tess couldn't have been too happy about that."

The others frowned and shook their heads hearing that.

"There was gossip that both Tess and Tina had affairs with Weir, and the police think that Weir dropped Tess when she got ill. When the real Tess went into remission, she decided to come home. She arrived the day before Halloween. She didn't tell her sister; she wanted to surprise her. She thought it would be fun to show up at the Halloween party.

"At some earlier point, Shay became suspicious of the pretend Tess. So did Stanley Cubbage. Tina wasn't worried about Stanley; he had a troubled history with the police. But Shay was a problem. She may also have been jealous of Shay's relationship with Weir. He had been Tina's lover occasionally also."

"Did Tina have MS too?" Rawley Sr. asked.

"No. She didn't need that wheelchair. It was part of the ruse. That was how she was able to sneak upstairs and into the medicine locker to steal morphine when no one was around. Poor Winnie Fields was under suspicion, but the police couldn't come up with enough proof that it was she who assaulted Rawley. They later found out that Tina's fingerprints were on the needle left next to him."

"So Tina, pretending she was Tess, stole morphine and murdered both Shay and Weir and tried to kill my father," Rawley Jr. said. "What was her motive exactly for killing Weir?"

"There's more than one possible motive. First, Weir would no longer have anything to do with her romantically. And he threw the real Tess over pretty quickly when she got sick. You know what they say about a woman scorned. Plus, Shay might have told Weir her suspicions about whether Tess was who she said she was."

"Okay, I think I've got that. Now why did Tina want to kill my father? And how did she get into his apartment?"

"By the back stairs, probably when everyone thought she'd gone home. This is a big place. I'll bet there are lots of secret passageways and closets. Not to mention doors to hide behind. As for your father, Shay had given the ledger pages to your father as well as giving them to Tess—or Tina—hoping she would corroborate Shay's suspicions. Maybe she thought Shay had also told your father her suspicions about Tess. Tina was trying to cover all the possibilities. The police also think Shay suspected Tina was impersonating Tess and hoped to blackmail Tina into keeping quiet about her and Weir."

"Oh my, what a mess!" Rawley Jr. said.

"So Tina," Emily continued, "killed Shay, who suspected Tina was impersonating Tess. She may also have been jealous of Shay's relationship with Weir. Next, she tried to kill Mr. Bingham."

"Wait! If Weir was her lover, why would Shay care if he was embezzling?" asked Rawley Sr.

"Perhaps she thought that was wrong. Having a relationship doesn't mean you excuse everything a person does. Besides, he wasn't just cooking the books. He stole Mr. Bingham's two hundred dollars and wrote fraudulent checks on the Dragos' account. People seem to think that Shay genuinely cared about the residents here."

Catherine and Rawley Sr. nodded at this.

"Remember, too, that Weir was married to Shay's sister, and we know he was in deep financial trouble. Perhaps Shay wasn't too happy to see her sister living in poverty, married to an embezzler and a cheat."

"Why did he need to embezzle?" Rawley Jr. asked.

"Because he had gambling debts," Catherine chimed in. "I saw him being escorted out of Delaware Park! He used my credit card information to pay his utility bills and stole one thousand dollars from the Dragos' checking account," Catherine replied.

"What about that blue Bic lighter found in Mr. Bingham's apartment?" Bob asked.

"Don't know," Emily said. "Perhaps Tina put it there to implicate Weir. If Rawley Sr. had found out Weir was embezzling, Weir would have had a motive to hurt him. We'll have to ask Detective Cortez if we ever see her again."

Everyone was quiet for a few moments, trying to follow all the threads of the plot in their mind.

"What has happened to Tina? Do you know?" Catherine asked.

"Cortez says she is being held for murder."

"And Tess?" asked Rawley Sr.

"I don't think they're charging her with anything," Emily said. "She might be back at work tomorrow."

"Who will fill in for the director?" Rawley Sr. asked.

"Harold Drago, I believe," Catherine said. "Nichole will take over Shay's duties until a replacement is found."

The room was silent for a moment as everyone considered this new information.

"More wine?" asked Rawley Sr., after refilling Catherine's glass.

"No more for me," Bob said. "I'm driving."

"And I'm quite tired," Emily added. "I think we should leave."

"I'm suddenly not feeling so well myself," Catherine said. "Walk me back to my apartment, Bob."

Catherine, Bob, and Emily rose to leave.

"Thank you," Rawley Jr. said. "Hopefully, things will calm down now. I'm going to try to talk my father into moving in with me until a new director is named."

"Don't even think about it," Catherine said, looking up at her son. "All my friends are here. And all the bad people have been caught."

"Ditto," said Rawley Sr. to Rawley Jr.

The trio left and walked down the hall to Catherine's door.

"No need to come in, I'm straight to bed," she said.

Bob bent down and kissed her.

"I'll call you tomorrow." Catherine smiled at Bob and Emily.

Bob and Emily trudged out to Bob's SUV. They spoke little. Each was reviewing the events of the previous evening in their minds, trying to understand the depressing violence of murder.

As they neared Emily's neighborhood, she said, "I think I know now what Letty was trying to tell me."

Bob didn't respond. He still wasn't comfortable with Emily saying she'd seen and spoken to a ghost.

Emily plowed on. "She told me to 'Beware the changeling.' That must have been Tina, who was masquerading as her twin, Tess."

"I guess," Bob replied. He was tired, too tired to rehash the murders and Emily's ghost story. Emily took the hint and didn't pursue it.

"See you at work tomorrow," Emily said, getting out of the car at her townhome.

"Okay" was all Bob said, but he waited until he saw Emily safely inside before he drove off.

CHAPTER TWENTY-EIGHT
Friday, November 2

Friday morning, 5 a.m., Emily's phone rang. She had hardly slept, but she jumped immediately out of bed to answer it.

"Hello?"

"Emily, it's Bob. They called an ambulance for my mother last night. She's in Chester County Hospital. They think she fell in her apartment."

"Oh, Bob, this is awful. Did she break her hip?"

"I don't know. They haven't told me anything yet. Look, why don't you call in sick today? That's what I'm going to do. Meet me at the hospital around ten. I'm there now, but I don't think they'll let nonfamily in until regular visiting hours."

Oh my, another mark against me with the managers, thought Emily. But there was no choice. She had to be with Bob and his mother.

"Will do. See you then."

She found Bob sitting on a molded plastic chair in a waiting area along the hallway on the fifth floor. She handed him a coffee from Dunkin' Donuts. She had brought one for herself too.

Bob kissed her and only commented, "My mom is being examined by about the fourth doctor, as far as I know. No one will tell me anything. I'm waiting to hear how she's doing." He started thinking of all the possible situations he might soon have to deal with: immediate surgery for his mother, months of rehabilitation, and managing all this. He gave up and decided he shouldn't worry until he knew the situation. Maybe she had only pulled a muscle or twisted something out of place. It didn't have to be a fracture.

Bob also remembered the hours and hours he spent at St. Francis Hospital when his father had passed away five years earlier. Then, he had brought a book to keep him company. Now, he was glad

Emily was there with him.

Emily had little experience sitting in hospitals and decided to stay quiet until Bob was ready to talk. She imagined he was very worried and thinking of all the worst-case scenarios. She was doing the same, thinking how sad it was that such an intelligent and vibrant woman should be so suddenly stricken.

"What are you thinking?" he finally asked Emily.

"Probably all the same things you're thinking," Emily responded. "But we really shouldn't worry until we've spoken to the doctor."

"You're right," Bob said. "I can't help it though."

"Me too."

In the stillness of the waiting area, they were suddenly surprised to see an elevator open and a hospital gurney with two orderlies and a nurse exit. They stopped in front of Bob and Emily. Catherine was lying there with her eyes closed. She appeared to be breathing, but she wasn't moving.

"Is she knocked out?" Bob asked in a panic. "She looks asleep, but she can't be."

"She's on her way for an MRI. They've given her a sedative," explained the nurse, who stayed behind while the orderlies exited.

"Your name is Nora?" Bob asked, pointing to the ID card she wore around her neck.

"Yes," she answered kindly. *What else would it be?* she wanted to say, but she kept that thought to herself, understanding his distress.

"Nora, why would they knock her out for an MRI?"

"They did it because she was in a lot of pain when she came in, and she wouldn't stop moving. We needed her to lie still."

"When will she wake up?" Emily interrupted.

"In thirty or forty minutes. Don't worry. This is standard procedure. The doctor will see you immediately after. Can I get you anything? A cup of coffee or a soda?" Nora asked them.

"No thank you," Bob replied.

"Me neither," Emily added.

"Then I need to get back to my duties," Nora said. "Please come by the desk if you need me." And she disappeared down the hall.

After twenty minutes, the orderlies and the gurney returned; Catherine was still unconscious. A young Indian doctor followed them. As the orderlies wheeled Catherine farther down the hall, the doctor stood before Bob and Emily, smiled, and introduced himself.

"I'm Doctor Singh, and I'll be looking after your mother. I have seen the MRI images; your mother has a broken pelvis. It's broken in three places." He paused for a moment to let them absorb that.

Neither Bob nor Emily was sure what to say.

"You are her family?" Singh asked next.

"I'm Bob, her son. This is Emily, my girlfriend. How did this happen, doctor?"

"It's difficult to say. Perhaps she fell or simply bumped hard into something like a dresser or a sink. Her bones are so brittle they cracked immediately. It's even possible they had already started disintegrating before she fell." He paused.

"So you can fix this, right?" Bob asked.

"Well, Bob, I'm afraid the news is not good." He paused again. Experience had taught him not to rush in with too much information too fast. Families rarely remembered more than a third of what he said the first time he said it. He understood. He had lost his own mother only the year before.

"So you'll operate?" Bob asked.

Doctor Singh shook his head sadly. "We cannot. There is a lot of internal bleeding, and your mother is too fragile for surgery." He stopped there.

"I don't understand," Bob said. His brain was numb. *What is this doctor trying to tell me?*

Emily thought she understood. She took Bob's hand.

"Dr. Singh," she said. "You're saying that you cannot operate and that there is internal bleeding. Are you saying that Mrs. Bowie is going to die?"

Bob looked up suddenly, a touch of anger in his eyes, but he kept quiet. He didn't trust himself to speak.

"Yes. There is nothing we can do. She weighs only seventy-eight pounds. She would not survive the anesthesia. But we will make her comfortable, and she will not suffer."

"What do we do now?" Emily asked. She glanced at Bob. He seemed frozen in shock. She shuddered, feeling a huge pang of pity for him.

"We will find a quiet room where she will be monitored and you can visit her. She should wake up soon. We will give her morphine for her pain..."

Emily finished the sentence in her head, *until she passes.*

"Thank you, doctor," Emily said. Bob remained silent. Doctor

Singh walked slowly away. Emily continued to hold Bob's hand as they sat in silence.

****

She knew the end was near. Surprisingly, there was no pain. She could feel her spirit slowly ebbing out of her body, very slowly, in small rivulets that flowed out from her hands and into the ether. She'd never thought it could take days, but here she was, three days in the hospital and still her body stubbornly clung to life.

Bob was there for hours, leaving only to go home to shower and rest. Emily was there, too—sometimes with Bob, sometimes alone. They read the newspaper to her and poetry, but she had no strength to speak to them. She couldn't even smile. She was in a twilight state between life and death and anxious to be gone.

The nights were so long. She'd awake and wish she were somewhere else. She thought of small children who insisted on going to bed at night with a teddy bear or doll. Like them, she needed something to draw comfort from. *Oh, Mosely,* she sighed, *if only you were here.*

In the early morning of the fourth day, when she was quite alone, Catherine Bowie fell into a light sleep for an hour then was woken up by a dog barking outside her hospital room door. "Now when did they start letting dogs in here?" she asked out loud.

At once, Mosely was there, sitting on the floor beside her bed. With a quick leap up, he landed on the bed and put his face up to hers. He nuzzled her softly. She was shocked to find the fur was still the soft polyester of her pretend Mosely, but he was moving and breathing. She touched his back and felt that it was warm to her touch. Tears welled up in her eyes, and she reached to hug him. Mosely responded and settled down on her chest while Catherine's thin arms hugged him to her. "Oh, Mosely," she whispered. "You are a real dog."

At the nurse's station, the staff was alerted to the monitor changes in Mrs. Bowie's room. An alarm sounded the emergency, and two nurses rushed to her room. The third nurse dialed a phone to summon the doctor on call.

They found Mrs. Bowie quiet and smiling with her arms around a large black stuffed dog.

"She's passed," noted one nurse and pointed to the DNR bracelet on Mrs. Bowie's wrist.

"Where did that dog come from?" the other asked.

"Who knows," said the first. "But I guess he came to take her home."

THE END

ABOUT THE AUTHOR

Maryellen Winkler, a native of Wilmington, Delaware, has been a lifelong lover of mysteries ever since reading her first Nancy Drew adventure. She is a graduate of the University of Delaware with a B.A. in English. She attends the Osher Lifelong Learning Institute, where she conducts a poetry workshop.

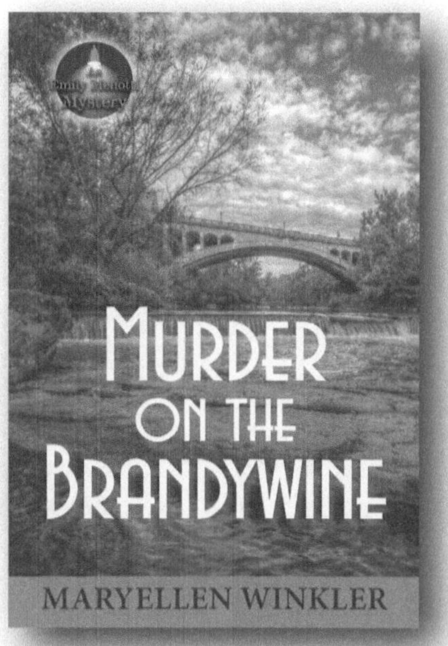

Intrepid amateur sleuth, Emily Menotti, is on her first Caribbean cruise along with the Wayward Sisters book club. As they head out of New York City, however, a friend goes missing.

With the help of her clairsentient pal, Melinda, Emily starts investigating. Yet even a séance, guided by Melinda, reveals more old secrets than new clues.

Set amid tropical backdrops, this mystery has motives aplenty, including an ex-husband, a former high school boyfriend, and the on-going resentment of two unmarried friends.

Join Emily as she solves the mystery on a chilling cruise with some uninvited passengers: jealousy, revenge, and death.

A beautiful young woman, Alicia Kingston, is on the verge of having her dreams come true. Engaged to be married, she is drawn into a revolutionary group that plans to strike a blow against the evils of the 1990s banking industry. But one Sunday morning, she is found murdered in Brandywine Creek State Park.

Mirety Bank, a major player in predatory lending practices, is Alicia's employer. Also working there is Emily Menotti, the woman who discovers Alicia's body. Is the mysterious tattoo of an owl on Alicia's back tied to her death? As Emily investigates, Alicia's fiancée, her brother, and higher-ups in the bank all become suspects.

Emily's search revives all her favorite memories of living in Wilmington and the Brandywine Valley. Follow in her footsteps as she tracks down the killer and ends up fighting for both her job and her life.

There's going to be a murder, or is there?

Emily and her friends are vacationing in Rehoboth Beach, Delaware. On their very first night, their sleep is disturbed by a woman screaming that someone is going to die. Angie Skinnard is staying next door in the haunted Chalet House, where tyrannical Mr. Skinnard is treating his adult children like servants. The siblings scramble to keep him happy and struggle to get along with each other for the long vacation week. Emily and Melinda, concerned that someone is in danger, befriend the family and try to learn their secrets.

Can they avert a tragic outcome?

EMILY'S PREVIOUS ADVENTURES

are available at

The Hockessin Bookshelf

The Newark Arts Alliance

The Palette and the Page

and Amazon.com

www.ingramcontent.com/pod-product-compliance
Lightning Source LLC
Chambersburg PA
CBHW020116310726
48970CB00002B/666